A Hoof in the Door

D1189044

By the same author

Eventer's Dream
Ticket to Ride

CAROLINE AKRILL

A Hoof in the Door

DRAGON
Granada Publishing

Dragon Books
Granada Publishing Ltd
8 Grafton Street, London W1X 3LA

Published by Dragon Books 1984

First published by Arlington Books Ltd 1982

Copyright © Caroline Akrill 1982

ISBN 0-583-30648-9

Reproduced, printed and bound in Great Britain by
Hazell Watson & Viney Limited,
Aylesbury, Bucks

Set in Times

All rights reserved. No part of this publication may
be reproduced, stored in a retrieval system, or
transmitted, in any form, or by any means, electronic,
mechanical, photocopying, recording or otherwise,
without the prior permission of the publishers.

This book is sold subject to the conditions that it
shall not, by way of trade or otherwise, be lent,
re-sold, hired out or otherwise circulated
without the publisher's prior consent in any
form of binding or cover other than that in
which it is published and without a similar
condition including this condition being imposed
on the subsequent purchaser.

For Elaine
in memory of a very similar accident

Contents

Contents

1

A Driving Ambition

'You don't think, Elaine,' Nigella Fane said in an enquiring tone, 'that The Comet is beginning to step out a bit?'

Almost before the words were out of her mouth, the dog cart hit a stone on the lane and bounced in the air. Nigella grabbed the side of the cart, and I snatched up the reins which had hitherto been lying unattended across The Comet's dappled rump. Lulled by the rhythmic clopping of hooves, the rumbling of wheels, the creaking of leatherwork, and the blissful warmth of the spring sunshine, I hadn't been paying any attention to the horse at all. I had been admiring the scenery, yet I had quite failed to notice that the scenery was slipping past at an accelerated rate.

I stood up in the cart and yanked the slack of the reins through the terrets. 'Steady boy,' I said warningly, 'slow down now.' But The Comet wasn't listening. His ears were set ominously for the way ahead and they didn't even twitch in my direction.

'I told you we should have fixed him with a bearing rein,' Henrietta Fane said in an irritated voice from the back seat. 'If he really gets going there'll be no holding him. You know what he's like.'

I knew only too well, since The Comet was my horse. I had foolishly accepted him in lieu of unpaid wages after an argument with the Fanes.

'People haven't used bearing reins since the days of Black Beauty,' I told Henrietta crossly. I hauled uselessly at The Comet's cast-iron mouth. 'They're probably illegal.'

'A pity,' Henrietta commented acidly, as the cart began to sway from side to side in a discomforting manner, 'because The Comet obviously needs one.'

I made no reply to this, being almost rocked off my

7

balance. I lurched back into my seat and wedged my feet firmly against the front of the cart in order to get a better grip on the reins. As I sawed furiously at the grey horse's Liverpool bit, I wondered if anyone else in the history of horsemanship had ever been run away with at the trot; because between the wide-banked ditches thick with cows-lips, under the vast and luminous East Anglian sky, The Comet was certainly running away now. His neck was set solid, his head was down, his rump was swinging in a determined manner, and his front legs were shooting out like pistons, achieving elevation and suspension worthy of a dressage horse.

'Perhaps you should try the brake,' Nigella suggested. Her voice was calm, but the knuckles of one hand showed white on the outside rail. With the other hand she clutched her hat. It was a small, red, satin pill-box with a polka-dot veil. Nigella considered it just the thing for driving.

I looked round for anything which resembled a brake. I had found the ramshackle cart in the gloom of the disused coach-house behind the stables at Havers Hall, where it had been mouldering away for decades. If it had ever had a brake, it certainly didn't have one now.

'There isn't a brake,' I said helplessly. 'There's nothing to control the speed with at all, apart from the reins.'

'Then kindly tell that to The Comet,' Henrietta yelped, 'because he doesn't appear to know, and I'm not enjoying this very much!' I wouldn't have changed even my own unenviable position for Henrietta's. She was riding with her back to us on a fragile little dickey seat suspended above the lane, with her feet jammed against a wobbly foot-rest.

By means of a herculean effort, I managed to get back on my feet in order to set the whole of my weight and strength against The Comet, leaning backwards on the reins like a Roman Charioteer. Eight stones and three pounds of dead weight did nothing to impede the grey horse's progress whatsoever, particularly as one of the reins snapped almost immediately. I hurtled backwards, almost knocking Henrietta off the dickey seat. Henrietta was still screeching when a car came round the bend.

The car braked furiously and skidded. It swerved out of our path and mounted the bank in a desperate and noble attempt to avoid taking off our outside wheel. As we bounced against the opposite bank, I caught a momentary glimpse of the driver's ashen face, before The Comet's iron-shod hooves carried us relentlessly on.

'I don't want to add to your troubles,' Nigella gasped, 'but the wheel on my side is behaving in a very peculiar fashion.'

I had time for one last despairing heave at The Comet's plank-like jaw, before being completely thrown off my feet by an appalling jolt and a rib-cracking rebound, followed by a prolonged splintering crash. The Comet, the lane, the banks and the sky seemed to spin round like a kaleidoscope, and when I opened my eyes again I was lying amongst the cowslips and the rogue wheel was bowling along the lane quite on its own and almost out of sight.

The Comet stood serenely on the tarmac attached to two broken shafts. Nigella, her pill-box slightly askew, stood at his head, surveying the remains of the dog cart which were scattered across the lane like kindling. 'Well,' she commented, as much to the horse as to anyone. 'That seems to be the end of that. I can't say I'm sorry.'

Henrietta scrambled up from the ditch, rubbing her elbow and looking murderous. Her anorak was split from top to bottom and her wild, waist-length hair was stuck with twigs and bleached grasses. I lay where I had landed, wondering if I would ever walk again, much less achieve my ambition to become a leading light in the world of the Three Day Event. When I had recovered sufficient nerve to move my head, I found myself facing a poster nailed to the trunk of a stag-headed oak.

The Midvale and Westbury Hunt
POINT-TO-POINT
April 25th

First Race at 2P.M.
Hon Sec O T V Bloomfield
Shrubbery Farm, Kettleton

I sat up, discovering with a flood of relief that I seemed to have retained the use of my limbs. 'Nigella,' I said urgently, 'I've just had an idea!'

Henrietta gave me a vicious look, She was examining a cut in her leg through a torn flap in her jeans, 'Well, if you wouldn't mind,' she said in a sour tone, 'we would prefer not to listen to it. Breaking The Comet to harness so that we could give driving lessons was your idea, if you care to remember, and it hasn't exactly been a roaring success; we might all have been killed.'

'Yes, quite honestly, Elaine,' Nigella said in a resigned tone, turning her attention from the shattered dog cart to the lacerated sides of her favourite satin-laced, tap-dancing shoes, 'it might be advisable to wait until we have recovered from the effects of this idea, before you suggest anything else.'

'But look at the poster,' I implored them. 'We could enter The Comet for the Point-to Point!'

There was a silence whilst the Fanes looked from me to the poster, to The Comet; then, 'How much money do you get if you win first prize at a Point-to-Point?' Henrietta asked.

'I don't know,' I admitted, 'but quite a lot I should imagine. Hundreds probably.'

'If we could win just enough to buy Legend a dressage saddle,' Nigella said thoughtfully, 'and some jump stands with proper cups and pins . . .'

'The Comet *must* have qualified,' I said. He's sure to be eligible. He's hunted for most of the season, and he goes like a bomb. Nothing, *nobody*, can catch The Comet once he gets into top gear.'

We all looked speculatively at the grey horse, weighing up his chances. The Comet was embarrassed to find that he had

10

suddenly become the centre of our attention. He raised his head in the unbecoming Liverpool bit and the blinkers, and he stared intently into the far landscape, as if he had unexpectedly caught a glimpse of someone he knew.

'But who will ride him?' Henrietta said. 'Which one of us will race?'

'Oh, I must,' I said firmly. 'After all, it's my event horse we are financing.'

This was not strictly true, because Legend was actually owned by the Fanes. They had bought him when they had realized that if I didn't find a sponsor to provide me with a potential event horse, I would leave them at a crucial time, when only our combined efforts had saved their floundering livery yard from bankruptcy.

'It can't be you, Elaine,' Nigella pointed out in her careful way, 'that wouldn't do at all. Imagine the consequences if you had an accident. If you broke an arm or a leg our event horse wouldn't have a rider and that would be the end of our sponsorship. No,' she decided, 'it will have to be me. I will ride The Comet.'

I didn't like the sound of this. It was true that Nigella had ridden The Comet more often than any of us, but while hunting last season, he had bolted with her and galloped straight into the river, practically drowning them both. I still saw Nigella's face in my nightmares, blanched and frozen, as the grey horse thundered unwaveringly towards the river bank.

'I think we'll forget about the Point-to-Point,' I said. Already I was sorry I had mentioned it.

But the Fanes had taken to the idea and they were not to be put off.

'We certainly *won't* forget about it,' Henrietta declared. She set about removing the broken shafts from the tugs on The Comet's driving pad. 'It's a stupendous idea! All Nigella has to do is sit tight and steer and let The Comet run himself out. Then she can pull up and collect the money.'

Even Nigella raised her eyebrows at this over-simplification of Point-to-Point racing. 'But at least I shall be racing over a properly laid-out course,' she said, 'and it will be properly organized and stewarded. It won't be at all like the rough-and-tumble of the hunting field.' She straightened her pill-box and slapped The Comet confidently on his neck. I knew from experience that there was no point in further argument.

We returned to the hall in ignominy, bowling the wheels of the cart like hoops, and leading The Comet up the pot-holey drive with his traces tied in knots at his sides like a farm horse returning from the fields. Against its backdrop of long-dead elms, Havers Hall looked grey and shabby in the sunshine. Its stucco was cracked, its brickwork was pitted, and its rows of windows were firmly shuttered against the rains of winter which had continued to seep in through the rotten woodwork.

The horses behind the sagging iron railings of the park raised their heads at the sound of the Comet's hooves. Ahead of them stretched a long idle summer of relaxation. There were three high-class horses belonging to our most valued clients, a pop group called Thunder and Lighing Limited. There was a thickset, pink-nosed, grey cob owned by Brenda, the Fanes' first-ever livery client, and there was a chestnut pony which belonged to our half-witted, part-time stable help, Doreen. Apart from the liveries, there were also the Fanes' own collection of cut-price, equine misfits, the hirelings, who were rented out during the season to unsuspecting clients who fancied a day with the Midvale and Westbury Hunt. They were all there, made fat and contented by the verdant spring grass; the mare-who-sometimes-slipped-a-stifle, the bad-tempered chestnut, Nelson, with his stitched-up eye socket, and the black-horse-who-never-stood-still. Amongst them I could see the dark bay gelding that was Legend, his summer coat already gleaming through on his shoulders and his flanks. I stopped and called to him, and after a moment of hesitation, he left the others and ambled lazily towards the fence.

12

I rummaged in my pockets and came up with a few damp and unworthy horse nuts. Legend ate them without enthusiasm, then screwed up the end of his nose in disgust, displaying a row of short, yellow teeth.

In the precious few months that I had known him, the good-looking bay horse had proved himself to be everything I had hoped for. I had no way of knowing if I would ever manage to break into the distant, expensive and exclusive world of the Three Day Event, but I did know that I had found the perfect horse with which to try. Legend was the embodiment of all my hopes and all my ambitions. Ambitions, I reflected with a twinge of misgiving, that Nigella and The Comet were about to risk their necks for.

2

A Few Pounds Short

'These fences,' Nigella commented, 'look a bit big from the ground.'

They did. Four feet of solid, black birch, as wide as they were high, in one instance flanked with a nine foot open ditch. Stouter hearts than Nigella's would have failed at the sight of them.

'If you're having second thoughts, there's still time to change your mind,' I told her. 'It isn't too late. We can easily scratch.'

We stood on the Point-to-Point course with our hands stuffed into the pockets of our anoraks and the ever-present East Anglian wind numbing our cheeks. All around us the Point-to-Point Committee and the Hunt Supporters' Club were busily engaged in raking up birch clippings and strapping hurdles together to act as wings. The Clerk of the Course, clad in ancient sheepskins and threadbare cords, was hammering in signs proclaiming WINNERS' ENCLOSURE, and FIRST, SECOND and THIRD; and in a convenient hollow below us which theoretically should have been out of the wind but somehow managed not to be, men in duffle-jackets fought the catering marquee, the canvas slapping and billowing like the sails on a galleon.

'There's no question of jibbing now,' Henrietta said sharply. 'The horse is qualified, fit and entered. We're not pulling out for anything.'

'As the owner of the horse, I think I'm entitled to make the decisions,' I pointed out, irritated by the way Henrietta had assumed control of the situation. 'It isn't actually your affair.'

'As the owner of the eventer we are supposed to be financing,' Henrietta snapped, 'it's more my affair than anybody's.'

14

'And as the rider of the horse, and the person who is more involved than either of you,' Nigella put in, 'I think you should both shut up.'

She set off resolutely to walk the course which consisted of sixteen fences over three and three-quarter miles of undulating flint-studded clay, her beautiful, brown hair streaming out from beneath a knitted purple helmet, pulled down firmly over her ears. Nigella was taking the race very seriously and had been out running before breakfast every day for a week. Henrietta and I trailed along behind, feeling unfit.

At the open ditch we came upon William and Nick Forster, the two young whippers-in to the Midvale and Westbury Hunt. They were armed with rammers, spades and a wheel-barrow, and they were working their way round the course, filling in holes.

'You're not serious about racing the old grey?' William pushed his cap to the back of his ginger thatch and stared at Nigella as if she was mad.

'I certainly am,' Nigella said. 'And what is more, I shall probably win.' She was dwarfed by the fences but her confidence was unshaken.

William was impressed but doubtful. 'Well, the old horse does have a fair turn of speed when he likes,' he allowed. 'He definitely can travel.'

'And he definitely can jump,' Henrietta added, launching herself down into the clay-walled ditch. 'He *never* stops. He's as brave as a lion.'

I looked at the dark, forbidding fence with the gaping yellow ditch behind it, and I thought that The Comet needed to be.

Forster didn't speak to us. He just continued to thump at a displaced sod of turf and he kept his face turned away. He had avoided me for several months after an embarrassing scene which had involved the Fanes. He made no secret of the fact that he thought I was crazy to work for them. He had wanted me to give in my notice, and he had even helped me find another job with a good wage and the prospect of an event horse thrown in. But the Fanes had foiled him by buying Legend, and I had lost the incentive to leave. I wanted to tell Forster that I had been grateful for his help and say that perhaps we could carry on where we had left off; but I didn't have the nerve, and anyway, the Fanes would have overheard. They disapproved of Forster because of his racy reputation, and considered him to be an unsuitable and unsettling influence.

So I stood, awkward and silent, whilst William kept a covert eye on Henrietta, who was his secret passion, and the Fanes in their knitted helmets energetically paced out the ditch in a snowstorm of kapok emerging from the split in Henrietta's anorak. The Fanes shopped for their clothes at *Oxfam* and *Help the Aged*. I wouldn't actually have liked to wear Nigella's white quilted ski-pants which didn't fit, and bagged at the seat, and had a lot of zippers in unexpected places, nor could I have worn Henrietta's electric-blue, satin disco trousers with black leg-warmers on top, but in my conventional groom's winter uniform of lovat-green Husky, cords and Hunter wellingtons, with my pale, straight, uninteresting hair stuffed under a tweed cap, I suddenly felt unutterably boring and drab. No wonder Forster wasn't interested in me. I turned to go, thinking that I would make my way back to the Fanes' delapidated shooting brake, when: 'How's the event horse, Elaine?' Forster asked.

'The event horse is OK,' I said, flustered, 'the event horse is fine.'

'Except that it's a little short of funds, and the Fanes have got to do damned fool-hardy things like racing the old grey to finance it.' Forster's voice was friendly enough, but the final thump he gave the turf was a vicious one.

'There isn't any cash,' I admitted. 'After the hunting season the income from the yard has dropped off to practically nothing.' There was no point in pretending. I tried not to look at Forster. I knew all about his rather

16

insolent mouth, the way his black hair curled over the back of his collar, and the thick curve of lashes over his blue eyes.

'And did you really expect that there ever would be any cash?' Forster enquired. 'Knowing the Fanes as you do, did you honestly expect it?' He threw the rammer at the wheel-barrow where it landed with an almighty crash. 'Honestly, Elaine,' he said in an exasperated voice, 'I said you were a fool to go and work for them in the first place, but I never imagined you would let them trap you into working for them for nothing for ever.'

Henrietta had noticed our conversation and immediately decided that it was time to leave. 'Elaine!' she shouted, 'we're going back to the car! Are you coming?'

'Anyhow,' Forster went on, as the spade clattered into the wheel-barrow beside the rammer, 'I hope you're going to try for the Hissey Scholarship this year.'

I waved at Henrietta to let her know that I would follow. 'Try for the what?' I said.

'Felix Hissey's training scholarship for event riders,' Forster said. 'He's always given a couple every year, but this year he's giving more, and it's being properly organized through the BHS. You have to be eighteen and have a promising young event horse to participate.' He paused and raised his shoulders. 'Well, you're eighteen, and you've got a promising young event horse . . .'

'I've also got the Fanes,' I pointed out, 'and Legend is their property, I can't just do as I like.' As if to reinforce this, there was a further shriek from Henrietta.

'*Elaine!*' she yelled. Do come *on!*'

'Anyway,' I said, remembering, 'Felix Hissey probably wouldn't even let me try for it; after all, I did turn down his job.'

'Turning down his job won't enter into it,' Forster said. 'Felix Hissey doesn't do the choosing any more, it's all done by the BHS, he just puts up the money.'

I had never seriously considered trying for a training scholarship before. Now it seemed to be the perfect solu-

17

tion. So perfect, in fact, that there just had to be a fly in the ointment somewhere, and I rather suspected that the fly would turn out to be the Fanes.

'I'll get you the details, anyway,' Forster said. 'I might be able to give them to you at the Point-to-Point.'

'But please don't say anything to the Fanes about it,' I begged him. 'I shall have to ask them first, and they might not like the idea.' I ran off up the course towards the Fanes, pleased on two counts. Forster was speaking to me again and there was a chance, if remote, of a training scholarship. Things were looking up.

On the way home we made a detour in order to visit *Help the Aged*, because Nigella needed a suitable jersey to race in.

'It's Mummy's duty day,' Henrietta said. 'She's sure to find us something.'

Lady Jennifer Fane was equally confident. 'But I *know* I shall be able to put my hand on the *very* thing!' she trilled. 'You can't imagine how many jerseys people bring to the shop, we turn away simply *hundreds*!'

She flung open several drawers, but all she could find was a pale green angora trimmed with a little pocket and a button.

'No, no,' Henrietta said. 'That won't do at all. We need a big, thick jersey with a stripe across the front or hoops on the sleeves.'

Lady Jennifer looked at us in genuine despair. She was tall and thin and highly strung, and she had Given Her Life to Charity. 'I'm *frightfully* sorry,' she said. 'I can't offer you *anything* with stripes or hoops.' We might have been customers in Harrods.

'We really need a man's jersey,' Nigella said. She flicked along a rail of dubious looking garments and discovered a pair of ginger velver knickerbockers. She pulled them out and surveyed them with admiration tinged with regret. 'Size eight! Could anyone possibly be that size?'

Lady Jennifer disappeared through a bead curtain and

18

returned bearing a red jersey of immense proportions. It was clumsily knitted and mis-shapen, but she laid it out on the glass-topped counter as if it was the finest cashmere. 'I really don't know if this would be of the *slightest* use to you at all,' she said. 'But it is the most *marvellously* warm colour, and I do have another in the most *heavenly* shade of blue'.

'What we really need is a two-tone jersey,' I explained. 'It's for the Point-to-Point. Nigella ought to have racing colours in red and blue to match the silks on my cross-country hat.'

Lady Jennifer had done her best, but now she looked defeated. A lot of wispy, grey hair had escaped from her unwieldy french pleat. 'I haven't got a red *and* blue jersey, Elaine,' she sighed, 'only a red jersey and a blue jersey.'

'I know what to do,' Henrietta declared. 'We can pull the sleeves off the red one, and fix them on to the blue one.' She leaned over the red jersey and picked experimentally at the sleeve join, to ascertain that all this was possible.

'Oh,' Lady Jennifer shrilled in alarm, 'I *really* don't think . . .'

'We'll buy them both,' Nigella interposed hastily, 'naturally.'

'And *naturally*,' I said in a low voice to Nigella, 'you have some money to pay for them, because I haven't.'

'It's all right,' Nigella said reassuringly, 'we can probably open an account.'

'We don't have accounts at *Help the Aged*,' Lady Jennifer said sharply.

'Perhaps we could do a swop then,' Nigella suggested. 'Your jerseys for ours.'

Lady Jennifer frowned. She wanted to help us, but her loyalty to The Cause was being severely stretched. 'Not Henrietta's,' she said firmly. 'Henrietta is so *frightfully* hard on jerseys. She picks at the wrists *constantly*; she always did, even as an *infant*.'

This proved to be true, because when Henrietta took off her anorak, her jersey was unpicked practically to mid-arm.

'Mine's all right anyway,' Nigella said. She pulled off her slightly discoloured Arran and replaced it with the red jumper. Apologetically, she added, 'We shall have to have yours as well, Elaine.'

I hadn't expected this. I was fond of my good navy guernsey. It had been a Christmas present from my father and I was loath to part with it.

'Come on, Elaine,' Henrietta said impatiently. 'Hand it over.'

Unhappily, I peeled off my Husky.

The Comet stood at the start of our improvised Point-to-Point course as if hewn from stone. With his noble bearing and his distinguished good looks, he could have been a top-flight steeplechaser. But Nigella, in the quilted ski-pants, to which, as a concession to horsemanship, she had added jodhpur boots frilled at the ankles with withered elastic, and a hard hat with a ventilator button missing, looked anything but a jockey.

Henrietta raised the flag, fashioned by means of a twig and a small, white, housemaid's apron, discovered during the ritual laying of rat-poison in the attics, and a legacy of the Fanes' former gentility.

'Once round,' she commanded, 'at half speed.' But it was clear, once the flag had dropped and the first furlong had been covered, the horse had other ideas.

The Comet galloped like an express train with an unrelenting thunder of hooves and his yellowing tail streaming like a banner behind him. He flew unerringly over the wild, untrimmed hedge, bore onwards in a wide half-circle across the park, and took, without the least falter in his stride, the log pile which was part of Legend's painfully built cross-country course. After this he made an unscheduled turn to the left, and despite Nigella's determined efforts to screw his head round to the right, he continued at a powerful speed towards the stable yard and the comfortable privacy of his own loose box.

20

'Henrietta,' I said, 'what happens if he does that tomorrow?' I thought of the network of lanes with their slippery tarmac, the jaunting gin-and-tonic traffic, and the fast-running river which had flooded its banks, all of which lay between The Comet and his stable; the stable where he stood like a statue for hours and hours and dreamed his mysterious dreams. Despite the fact that the grey horse was lofty and self-absorbed, and feigned indifference to man or beast, or perhaps even because of it, I felt something catch hold of my heart and give it a little twist.

'How can it possibly happen tomorrow?' Henrietta said scornfully. 'He's hardly likely to make a bolt for home, because he won't know which direction to take; he won't know where he is! After all,' she added, as she tossed away the twig and tied the apron round her waist with a flourish, 'he isn't a homing pigeon.'

We slung The Comet's saddle from the spring balance we used for weighing hay nets in the barn. It weighed twenty-five pounds. Nigella had weighed herself on the scales outside the village chemists, and even with five extra jumpers and her long riding boots, she couldn't make more than nine stone two pounds. The starting weight, which included the saddle, irons, leathers, girth and breastplate, was eleven and a half stones.

'Weights,' I told them. 'We shall be expected to provide weights.'

'What sort of weights?' Henrietta wanted to know.

'The sort of weights you carry when you're eventing,' I said. 'In a weight cloth with pouches on each side, and straps to attach it to the saddle.'

'What are they made of, these weights?' Nigella wondered.

'Lead,' I informed them. 'Lead pipe normally, you cut it up into pound and half-pound pieces, and then you hammer them flat.'

'We haven't any lead pipe,' Nigella said, dismayed. 'I'm sure of it.'

'Can't we use something else?' Henrietta suggested. 'Sugar or something?'

We lapsed into giggles, thinking of The Comet struggling round the Point-to-Point course with panniers full of sugar packets.

'There must be *something* else we can use,' Henrietta said.

'No,' I assured her, 'it has to be lead.'

Nigella subsided on to a convenient hay bale. She looked weary and oddly rounded in all the jerseys, topped off by the awful blue one with the red sleeves. 'Where on earth are we going to get lead from, at this time of night?' she sighed.

We all fell silent, thinking about it, then: 'I think I know,' said Henrietta, and she vanished into the darkness with a torch.

'I expect she's seen a piece of pipe lying around somewhere,' Nigella said, but when Henrietta returned, it wasn't with a piece of pipe.

Where she had found the wide strip of lead flashing with the prettily scalloped edges, neither Nigella or I thought fit to enquire. But the next time it rained, I noticed that the little portico with the doric columns and the pointed roof which sheltered the main entrance to the hall leaked like a sieve.

3

A Maiden's Race

There was a flurry of race-cards as I led The Comet into the paddock.

'Hold on a minute, miss!' A steward ran after me in order to tie a number on my arm. He looked at The Comet in admiration. 'Nice horse, miss,' he said, 'got a powerful hindquarter on him.'

The powerful hindquarter was the result of dragging half a tree round the park as part of being broken to harness, but there was no time to go into this with the steward. 'You mind you don't get him kicked, miss,' he warned. 'Some of these beggars are over the top.' Other horses were piling up behind. One of them ran backwards and stood on end, pulling the leading-rein out of its attendant's grasp. There was a short interval of chaos until it was recaptured.

I led The Comet along the inside of the rails. Some of the other runners in the Ladies' Race were already parading, sidling along with their tails up, rolling their eyes and snatching at their bits, upset by the atmosphere of excitement, the proximity of the jostling crowd, and the hoarse shouts of the bookmakers. The Comet was unmoved by it all. He stalked along, looking regal. People looked him up hastily as he passed them by.

'Good-looking grey, what's its number?'

'Grand sort of animal that.'

'Number twenty-two. The Comet.'

'My God,' somebody else exclaimed, aghast. 'It's the Fanes' old grey! It's unstoppable!'

In the middle of the paddock, Nigella waited in her red and blue. Henrietta stood beside her with the saddlery. She looked unfamiliar and even vaguely fashionable in one of Lady Jennifer's ancient tweed suits which dated from the

23

New Look. When the steward had finally managed to get all the runners forward, he waved us in to saddle up. There were nine runners, all bays and chestnuts. The Comet was the only grey.

Nigella looked pale but composed. She pulled off the paddock sheet and Henrietta put on the weight cloth, followed by the number cloth and the saddle. The Comet stood like a statue whilst I reached under his belly for the girths.

'Some of the others look a bit hot,' Nigella remarked, taking in all the plunging and snorting going on around us.

'With a bit of luck they'll wear themselves out before they get to the start,' Henrietta said. 'I reckon Mrs Lydia Lane's horse is the one to watch.'

Mrs Lydia Lane's horse was a massive foam-flecked bay, who pinned his ears back and lashed out as a groom pulled up the surcingle. Mrs Lydia Lane wore beautiful calf boots with silky trousers tucked into them like a Cossack, and a dark and glossy fur coat. She looked very glamorous.

'No wonder Nick Forster found her so attractive,' Henrietta commented.

I didn't rise to this, being engaged in replacing the paddock sheet.

'It was the talk of the county, at the time,' Henrietta went on. 'There was quite a scandal. I do believe that her husband threatened to shoot him.'

'I don't know why you are telling me all this,' I said, flipping The Comet's tail over the fillet string. 'It isn't as if I'm actually interested.'

'Oh,' Henrietta said innocently. 'I thought you were.'

It was not the moment to fall out with Henrietta. I led The Comet back into the walk-round. He may have been a bolter, but he was mine, and I was proud of him. He had taken everything in his implacable stride; the early preparation, the journey, the arrival and the unfamiliar surroundings, the noise and the bustle of the course; and now he sailed round the paddock with the demeanour of one who

24

paraded in public every day of his life. He looked a wise, experienced, sensible and powerful horse, in fact just the kind the punters tend to fancy for the Ladies' Race. He had no breeding entered on the race-card, no impressive thorough-bred blood-lines, and no previous form whatsoever. He was just *The Comet. Grey Gelding. Breeding unknown. Aged.* But already the odds were shortening on the Tote from rank outsider to 8-1 against.

Buoyed up by the general excitement and the sense of occasion, I had lost most of my former uneasiness about the Point-to-Point, but now, through a gap in the crowd, I saw the winner of the last race being led down to the horse-boxes with distended nostrils, pumping sides and lowered head. His neck was black with sweat and there was blood on one of his hind legs. I was suddenly terribly afraid for The Comet.

'Turn your horses in please!' the steward shouted. Every-one stopped on the perimeter of the ring and turned their horses' heads to the centre. Up on the number frame, Nigella's name and The Comet's number had appeared. Henrietta removed the paddock sheet for the last time and tightened the girths. She legged Nigella into the saddle. Nigella's hands were trembling as she took up the reins, but she still managed to give me a reassuring smile. 'It'll be all right,' she said. 'Really.'

Outside the paddock I unclipped the leading-rein and pulled it through The Comet's snaffle rings. 'Nigella,' I pleaded, 'do take care. Please don't take any chances.'

Mrs Lydia Lane's horse flew past us with an enormous bound which nearly unseated its jockey. Next to The Comet, the rider of a raw-boned chestnut took out her teeth and handed them to her attendant for safe-keeping. The hunts-man, dressed in his scarlet with brass buttons flashing in the sunlight, rode forward to lead the parade of runners on to the course.

'Good luck!' Henrietta shouted after Nigella. 'Make sure you're the first back!' She was bright-eyed and flushed with excitement. In contrast, Nigella looked cool and determined.

25

Mrs Lydia Lane's horse was the first to canter away towards the start, shaking its head, scattering froth like snow. The Comet cantered steadily; it was easy to distinguish the grey with the red and the blue.

'We'll find a good place to watch from,' Henrietta said in an agitated voice.'Over there, up on the rise! We should be able to see the whole course from there!' She set off towards the rise at a run, dodging through knots of people.

'Here,' Forster's voice said. 'You might need these.' He gave me some papers which I stuffed into my pocket, and he put a pair of binoculars into my hands. I tried to thank him, but he was gone, jumping into the Hunt Land Rover which bucketed after the runners to take up its position on the course.

I ran after Henrietta. My heart felt like a stone in my chest. I knew that horses were irretrievably injured at Point-to-Points, that in the back of the Hunt Land Rover there were green canvas screens put up to spare the feelings of the crowd; and that afterwards the owners went home with empty lorries and broken hearts. At that moment I loved The Comet more desperately than I had ever loved anything in the world, and I couldn't bear the thought of losing him.

'Henrietta,' I cried wretchedly. 'What if something awful happens?'

But Henrietta was beyond hearing. 'They're calling the roll,' she exclaimed, 'they're all lined up. The Comet's in the middle. They've already called Nigella, I saw her turn her head!'

The loudspeaker above our heads crackled into life. 'They're under starter's orders,' the commentator said.

Below us, beside the uneven line of fidgeting horses with the black fences stretching in front of them I saw the white flag rise. My heart started to pump violently, the flag dropped, and suddenly all the horses were galloping towards the first fence. The Comet was in the middle of a tight bunch. I didn't know much about Point-to-Pointing, but I knew that this was the worst possible place to be. I could imagine the thunder of hooves to the front, to the sides and behind. I could see the huge, black fence looming nearer with no room for error, yet with no possible way to see a stride into it. I closed my eyes and in the next few seconds my heart stopped beating altogether and I probably stopped breathing as well.

'They're all over the first,' the commentator said.

Henrietta grabbed the binoculars. 'He's lying third . . . It's a good place to be! Keep him steady, Nigella . . . Hold him back . . . They're spreading out a bit, good . . .'

I couldn't bear to watch, but then on the other hand, I couldn't bear not to. I saw the bunch of horses swing round to the next fence; they were not so close together now. The leaders jumped, one, two, and then the grey horse sailed over and made a perfect landing. The next horse fell. Uniforms appeared out of the crowd and carried off the jockey without the teeth. The raw-boned chestnut galloped gamely after the field, reins and stirrups flying.

'He's dropped to fourth,' Henrietta said with disappointment in her voice, 'the others are overtaking him.'

The line of horses, strung out like a necklace, took the open ditch without mishap and completed the first circuit. At the next fence another horse fell. It scrambled to its feet and shook itself like a dog before setting off towards the horse-box park with several spectators in hot pursuit. The jockey limped back down the course, shaking her head at the St John's Ambulance Brigade. Mrs Lydia Lane's bay was going strongly in the lead, it looked a sure winner, and half way round the second and last circuit The Comet had fallen back to sixth.

'At least he's all right,' I breathed, 'even if he isn't going to get a place, he looks as if he's going to finish the course safely.'

'Don't underestimate his chances,' Henrietta said, 'he's coming up!'

And The Comet was coming up! Now he was fifth, and

27

suddenly he was fourth! Even from so far away it was plain to see that The Comet had taken the race into his own hands. Nigella was a mere passenger. She could no more hold him back than she could have held back a ten-ton truck with the brakes off. As we watched, the grey horse's stride settled into the familiar relentless gallop, the powerful hindquarters went to work, the iron neck stretched out; The Comet was away!

'He's third!' Henrietta yelled. 'He's second!'

'But he'll never catch the bay!' I screeched. 'He'll never do it!'

The crowd had begun to shout as Henrietta and I raced pell-mell down the side to the finish. We were there in time to hear the thunder of approaching hooves as the bay come round the bend, stretched out at a flying gallop, and coming up behind him was The Comet. On and on came The Comet with his raking stride, on and level with the bay, and as the crowd roared their approval, on and on came the grey and the blue and the red, into the lead and past the finishing post. But as Henrietta clutched my arm and screamed, 'He's won!' The Comet galloped on and over the black birch fence, and was galloping away over the next, with Nigella glued helplessly to the saddle like a wet rag.

'And it's the grey, it's number twenty-two, The Comet, with number eighteen in second place, and number twenty-five third . . .' the commentary tailed off in an uncertain manner. 'I have got it right, haven't I?' the commentator was heard to say. 'This was the second circuit?'

The crowd was flabbergasted. The cheers died on their lips. 'Oh, *no!*' Henrietta shrieked in despair. 'Stop him, Nigella! Stop him! You've got to weigh out! We'll be *disqualified!*'

The rest of the runners had pulled up and were staring in consternation after The Comet. Some looked uncertain as to whether or not they should follow.

'She's gone on,' Mrs Lydia Lane's jockey said, 'I'm going

to lodge an objection.' She turned the dripping bay and rode away towards the steward's tent.

Henrietta and I stood as if frozen to the ground, and all around us the arguments raged.

'If the horse has won, it's won, and that's that!'

'No, it has to weigh out immediately afterwards. If the jockey doesn't weigh out, the horse is disqualified. You can't argue with the rules!'

'The rules say the winner's the first horse past the post, there's no rule that says it can't go on to jump a few more fences if it wants to!'

'I tell you the prize will go to the bay, the grey will be disqualified, although if you ask me, it's a damned shame . . .'

Suddenly though, unbelievably, there was an out-burst of delighted clapping and The Comet appeared, cantering back up the course, with Nigella still in the saddle. 'Sorry,' she panted apologetically. 'Couldn't stop. Had to run him into a thicket.'

I grabbed The Comet by his bridle and ran with him towards the steward's tent. The crowd surged along beside us determined to see fair play. Outside the tent Mrs Lydia Lane's jockey was haranguing the chief steward who had refused to accept her objection on the grounds that a 'reasonable period of time' had not yet elapsed. The Comet had not been disqualified. He was cheered and applauded all the way to the winners' enclosure.

Nigella slid down from the saddle and fell against the hurdles. She was wet with sweat and her face was as red as her jumper. She staggered through the well-wishers towards the weighing-out. Somebody threw a rug over The Comet. The grey horse was steaming like a turkish bath. His nostrils were lined with vermilion and every vein stood out in high relief. His breath came in huge, sobbing gulps. I was never so proud of anything or anybody in the whole of my life.

The weighed-out signal was given, and Nigella appeared beside us with the saddlery. We walked The Comet slowly back to the horse-box. Henrietta pressed her face against his sodden neck. 'I never imagined,' she said, 'that any horse of ours would ever win a Point-to-Point.'

'Any horse of mine,' I corrected her.

'What did you say?' Henrietta said, releasing The Comet.

'Any horse of mine,' I repeated, 'The Comet belongs to me.'

'Well,' Henrietta said dismissively, 'in a manner of speaking.'

'More than in a manner of speaking,' I said. 'I took The Comet instead of wages. You didn't want him. You were going to send him to Leicester Sales without a warranty. He would have ended up being knackered.'

'Never mind about all that,' Nigella said hastily. She removed The Comet's bridle and put on his headcollar. 'Where did you get the binoculars?'

'Oh,' I said, remembering, 'they belong to the Hunt.' I also remembered the papers in my pocket. I knew what they must be. Sooner or later I would have to tackle the Fanes about the scholarship, but not now, not today.

We sponged The Comet with warm water and disinfectant, and dried him with old towels. He let out a long, shuddering sigh and rubbed his face against Henrietta's tweeds. 'Whoever would have thought,' she commented, with a sly, sideways glance at me, 'that any horse of Elaine's would have won a Point-to-Point?'

4

Training the Event Horse

'Two hundred and seventy pounds is an awful lot of money for a dressage saddle,' Henrietta said. 'It's a *fortune.*'

We sat at the table in the flagged kitchen, nursing mugs of coffee. It was the evening of the day after the Point-to-Point, the time of reckoning. It was already dark outside the curtainless, stone-mullioned windows, and in the dusty iron chandelier above our heads three lights burned out of twelve.

'But if we are going to buy one,' Nigella reasoned, 'it may as well be the best.' She flipped through the pages of *Training the Event Horse* which she had ordered from the local library and adopted as her Bible. *'A badly-made dressage saddle can not only place the rider in the incorrect position, but also unbalance and affect the movement of the horse . . .'* she quoted. 'We don't want that to happen, do we?'

'No-o,' Henrietta allowed reluctantly. 'But all the same, two hundred and seventy pounds!'

'I agree that we need to buy a good one,' I said, 'but I don't see why it can't be second-hand. As long as it fits Legend properly, I think one that has been used a bit would be just as good as a new one, if not better.'

'Why didn't I think of that?' Henrietta leaned in front of us and grabbed the current issue of *Horse and Hound.* She turned to the classified advertisements, and as she perused them, she chewed a piece of her hideously tangled hair. 'Of course, just because we happen to want one, there won't be a second-hand saddle to be had.' She was right. There wasn't.

'Then we'll advertise for one,' Nigella decided. 'If we can get one for a hundred and fifty pounds, we will still have enough for the jump stands and the cups and pins.' She went off in search of pen, paper and envelope.

The Event Horse Training Fund had done well out of the Point-to-Point. The first prize for the Ladies' Race had been a hundred pounds, and as we had each speculated five pounds on The Comet for an outright win, our winnings on the Tote had amounted to another one hundred and thirty-five pounds.

Nigella returned with a piece of damp, cockled crested notepaper and a pen. Together we drafted a brief advertisement TOP QUALITY ENGLISH OR GERMAN DRESSAGE SADDLE WANTED, GOOD CONDITION. URGENT. This was followed by our address. Short as it was, it still set the Training Fund back almost ten pounds.

All day I had been waiting for a suitable moment to broach the tricky subject of the Hissey Scholarship. Now I took the details out of my pocket and put them on the table.

'That's a very official-looking document,' Henrietta said at once, eyeing the application form in a suspicious manner. 'I hope it isn't anything to do with our sponsorship. We did agree that it was to be a personal arrangement. We're not going to sign anything.'

'It's nothing like that,' I assured her. 'It's just something I want to discuss with you both. It's the details of the Hissey Training Scholarship.'

'Hissey?' Nigella said, looking up from writing the envelope. 'You mean Felix Hissey?'

'Yes,' I said, 'he awards a scholarship every year to six of the most promising young event riders and their horses. I rather thought we might try for it.'

'We?' Nigella said guardedly. 'Of course, what you actually mean to say is "you".'

'Now wait a minute,' Henrietta said heatedly. 'That 's just another form of sponsorship; you don't need another sponsor, you've got us.'

I had known it was going to be difficult; that the Fanes would want to do things in their own way. 'But Legend and I

32

are going to need professional help if we are to make any progress at all,' I told them, 'and the scholarship provides for a whole month's training with one of the very top international instructors. It's the chance of a lifetime.'

'And who's going to do your work whilst you are away on this whole month's training with a top international instructor?' Henrietta demanded to know. 'We can't possibly spare you for a month; we wouldn't be able to manage. It's out of the question.'

'The course is held in the spring,' I pointed out. 'After the hunting season; it's never a busy time.'

'Oh,' Henrietta said grumpily, not in the least mollified. '*Is* it.'

'The thing is,' Nigella said in a reasonable tone, 'that surely we can pay for professional tuition as and when we need it? After all, that's what our fund raising scheme is for.'

'I don't think you realize,' I said patiently, 'quite how much professional tuition costs.'

'I don't think we want to be bothered with Felix Hissey and his scholarship,' Henrietta said firmly. 'We can make it on our own.'

'Profession tuition,' I went on, 'costs about twenty pounds an hour.'

Henrietta choked on her coffee. '*How* much!'

'I did warn you how much it would cost to produce an event horse,' I reminded her. 'You knew it wouldn't be cheap.'

'I didn't expect it to be cheap,' Henrietta spluttered, 'but twenty pounds!' She turned an incredulous face to Nigella. 'We seem to have chosen the wrong business; we shouldn't be hiring out hunters at twenty pounds a day, we should be training eventers at twenty pounds an hour!'

'We could be,' I said, 'if we are successful at training this one. But you have to prove that you have the ability first, you have to have some form behind you.'

'You're right about that, anyway,' Nigella said. She opened *Training the Event Horse* at a page of photographs.

33

They showed Trisha Phillpotts during her early eventing successes with Fly On Brightly, then later, instructing potential, young event riders and horses.

'How many hours of professional tuition are you going to need?' Henrietta wanted to know.

'How can anyone possibly tell?' I said airily. 'Two, three, five or six hours a week.'

'Oh, goodness,' Nigella gasped, 'surely not.' She turned over the pages of her Bible to ascertain if this could be so.

'She's kidding us,' Henrietta said. 'What does the book say?'

'Of course, if you still think we can manage to pay for it,' I continued, 'there's no point in even considering the scholarship.'

'Now, let's not be too hasty,' Henrietta said. 'We may as well keep our options open.'

'*Professional training and advice are essential to the potential event horse and rider,*' Nigella read. '*Expert training can take a less than brilliant combination to the top, the lack of it will prevent even the most gifted horse and rider from achieving their potential.* You can't argue with that,' she concluded.

'Perhaps we should just consider the *possibility* of a scholarship,' Henrietta suggested. 'I mean, as Elaine already had the details, we may as well see what Felix Hissey has to offer.'

I spread the sheets out on the table. 'What he has to offer is a month's course with a top international instructor, all expenses paid . . .'

'When you say all expenses,' Nigella enquired, 'do you mean everything; tuition, food and lodging for the rider, and keep for the horse?'

'Yes,' I said, 'everything.'

'So it's worth quite a lot,' she said pensively, 'if you work it out at twenty pounds an hour.'

'About a thousand pounds,' I said.

'A thousand pounds!' Henrietta exclaimed. 'Glory!'

'Of course,' I said, 'if you still think it isn't worth trying for, if you're still not interested . . .'

'Read on,' Henrietta commanded. 'We're interested.'

'First of all you have to make a provisional entry on the form supplied, giving full details of yourself, your previous experience, and your horse. Then, if your entry is accepted, you are invited to go to a combined training competition, where the selection committee make a short list of prospective candidates.'

Nigella turned to the index of *Training the Event Horse* in order to look up combined training.

'It means dressage and show-jumping,' I informed her, 'at a fairly basic level.'

'That wouldn't be a problem,' Henrietta said, 'would it?'

'Well,' I said doubtfully, 'if we get the dressage saddle and jump stands . . .'

'No,' Henrietta decided, 'it wouldn't be a problem.'

'After that, the short-listed candidates take part in a mini-event held over two days. The selection committee watch the candidates schooling and competing, and then they make their final decision. They announce the names of their six chosen scholarship candidates at the end of the competition.'

'Do you have to pay anything for the two-day event?' Nigella said cautiously.

'No,' I said, 'it's completely free for the short-listed candidates.'

'And do you have to pay an entry fee to apply in the first instance?' she asked.

'No,' I said, 'that's free as well.'

'Then it seems to me that we can't afford not to try for it,' said Nigella.

Now that they had made a decision in favour of the scholarship, the Fanes began to panic in case something should prevent our participation. Nigella handed me the pen. 'Fill in the application form, Elaine,' she urged. 'When is the closing date of entry?'

'When's the combined training competition?' Henrietta said, anxiously craning over my shoulder. 'Do we have enough time to prepare?'

'And what do we need to be able to go,' Nigella said in an agonized voice, 'apart from the dressage saddle and the jump stands?'

'The combined training is next month,' I told them, and added that we would need another saddle, suitable for cross-country and show-jumping. I could make do with the rugs, rollers and bandages we already had, but Legend would also need a double bridle; there wasn't a double bridle in the yard, and even the snaffle bridle I was using for schooling was pulled up to the top holes, and the bit was almost an inch too wide.

'So even if we get the dressage saddle and the jump stands with the money we already have,' Nigella mused, 'we still need another saddle and bridle, which will cost us almost as much again.'

'I could use one of the old hunting saddles,' I said. 'Even the one I'm using now would do at a pinch, but it's very straight in the seat, and not at all forward cut. It isn't really built for the job.' I didn't add that the stirrup leathers had a distressing tendency to fly off backwards when Legend took one of his unexpected, exaggerated leaps, and that the girth straps were cracked and withered.

'You can't go without the proper equipment,' Nigella said, 'it would look unprofessional, and I'm sure it would affect your performance.' She thumbed through *Training the Event Horse* until she came to the chapter on saddlery. '*A general purpose saddle with a reasonably deep seat and knee and thigh rolls, is essential for the comfort and safety of both rider and horse*,' she read.

'So we shall have to do a bit more fund raising,' Henrietta declared. She jumped up and vanished into the squalid little scullery which served as our office and returned with a folded schedule which she placed triumphantly upon the table. 'And Rendlesham Horse Show might be just the place to do it!'

36

'Rendlesham Horse show?' Nigella said, interested. 'Might it really?'

I looked at the schedule, not at all sure that Rendlesham Horse Show was a good idea. Henrietta leaned over my shoulder and flipped back her hair, giving the programme of events her very closest attention.

'We can enter the mare-who-sometimes-slips-a-stifle in the ladies' hunter class,' she decided. 'That's fifty pounds, and another fifty if she wins the championship . . .'

'She couldn't win the championship,' Nigella objected, 'not possibly. The bigger horses always win.'

'And the bad-tempered chestnut in the riding horse class,' Henrietta went on. 'He may not always go very sweetly, but no one could deny that he's exactly the right stamp . . .'

'But the bad-tempered chestnut's coat isn't through,' I said. 'We were saying only this morning how terrible he looks.'

'And look at this!' Henrietta's finger stabbed at the schedule. 'A working hunter class! It's just the thing for Legend; and look at the prize money – seventy five pounds, *and* a trophy. We could sell it, it might be worth hundreds!'

'You can't sell a perpetual challenge trophy!' Nigella crid in horror. 'It has to be given back after a year!'

'But you must enter the working hunter class, Elaine,' Henrietta insisted. 'After all, it could be regarded as part of your training.'

This was true. It would be good experience for Legend to jump in the ring, and the fences would be soundly constructed, solid and natural. I resigned myself to some fairly blatant pot-hunting. Nigella was already filling in the entry form. 'Pity we haven't got a horse who can really jump,' she said, thoughtfully, 'the prize money is so much better.'

'But then we would have to join and register with the BSJA,' I pointed out, 'otherwise you can't compete.'

'That's true,' Nigella agreed, 'it's best to stick to the show classes.'

Henrietta picked up the schedule and sat down in her

chair, still perusing it. 'Did you notice that there's a private driving class?' she said. 'I don't suppose . . .'

'No,' Nigella said flatly. 'Certainly not.'

'We've done with driving,' I said. 'We haven't a vehicle any more, and anyway, The Comet's done his bit for the Training Fund.'

'Ah, well,' Henrietta said regretfully, 'as you wish.'

5

Show Business

'Will exhibitors in class five, ladies' hunter, mare or gelding, please make their way to the collecting ring?'

As the announcement was relayed across the show-ground, I secured Nigella's coiled-up hair with a couple of long pins, helped her to fit the veil over the brim of the silk hat, and pinned on to her lapel the smallest of creamy yellow roses to match her primrose waistcoat. The result was absolutely stunning. The navy side-saddle habit, cut narrower in the sleeve, tighter in the waist, and longer in the apron than was now quite fashionable, had belonged to Lady Jennifer when, in her youth, she had ridden with the cream of Leicestershire.

Henrietta looked up from the mane of the mare-who-sometimes-slipped-a-stifle with a plaiting needle in her mouth. 'Where's that fool, Doreen, with the numbers?' she managed to say. 'She's going to make us late.' She stuck the needle in her jersey and stood on tip-toe in order to nip the dangling piece of thread from the very last plait with her teeth.

Doreen appeared at my side as she spoke, trailing numbers and white tape and looking gormless. She was a thin, pale schoolgirl with a floppy page-boy haircut, who helped out in the stables whenever she could in return for the part-livery of her chestnut pony. '*Every*body's here,' she informed us, 'even the hunt. That Mister Forster, Elaine, he wanted to know if you was here. I told him you was.'

'You were supposed to have been running an errand for us, not gossiping with the hunt,' Henrietta said irritably, turning over the numbers and squinting at the secretary's crabbed writing to discover which was to be attached to Nigella.

I heaved the suede-seated side-saddle on to the mare-who-sometimes-slipped-a-stifle and wondered if I would have an opportunity to talk to Forster. He would be pleased, I knew, to hear that I had posted off my application form for the Hissey scholarship.

We put Nigella up on to the saddle, straightened her apron, and snapped the elastic over her boot. She pulled up the mare's girths as we set off through the horse-boxes towards the flags and marquees which surrounded the main ring.

Rendlesham Horse Show was held in a clearing hewn out of the forest, and the air was filled with the scent of resin and the sharpness of the sea. Years of falling pine needles had left the ground dry and naturally resilient, carpeted with short, soft grass, and the result was a perfect all-weather riding surface.

The bay mare arched her glossy neck with its border of tight, black plaits, and lengthened her stride, appreciating the going. As we had expected, there was not another horse in the collecting ring that could hold a candle to her.

'She's sure to win,' Henrietta muttered, 'providing the leg holds out.'

Inside the ring the two hunter judges signalled that they were ready to being. Nigella, displaying a smart piece of showmanship, managed to be first inside the rails.

It was years since I had been to a horse show. I stood at the ringside with Doreen and Henrietta, drinking in the half-remembered sights and the smells and the sounds of it; the elegant hunters walking out in front of the sparkling white rails, the banks of spring flowers around the grand-stand, the huge marquees, and the row of little trade-stands with their pennants fluttering angrily in the breeze. The ground vibrated with the thud of hooves, and from an adjacent ring came the regular crash of show-jumping poles accompanied by sympathetic moans from the crowd who stood six deep at the ropes. From the members' tent came the muted sound of laughter and the chink of glasses, and

40

the occasional whiff of beer mingled with the scent of pine and bruised turf and the heady tang of the sea.

Just as the ladies' hunters were about to be waved on into a trot, everyone was asked to hold back in order to accommodate a late arrival.

'Oh, no,' Henrietta exclaimed in disgust, 'it's the landlord's daughter.'

The landlord's daughter was Janie Richardson, who hunted with the Midvale and Westbury, and was greatly admired both for her looks and the quality of her horses. Her father was a rich publican, and her most striking feature was a mass of coal-black hair permed into a vast and solid frizz. It was a miracle that the frizz managed to fit under a silk hat, but she had flattened it down somehow and imprisoned it into a bun at the back of her neck, although as she trotted past us, I saw that fetching little spirals had drifted onto her blush-tinted cheeks. The landlord's daughter was very pretty in a stagey sort of way, but she was not beautiful like Nigella, nor as elegant, but Henrietta groaned. 'If there's any horse that could match up to the bay mare,' she said, 'it's Janie Richardson's Summer Nights.'

When Janie Richardson had found a space, the hunters were allowed to trot on, and the judges gave their attention to Summer Nights. He was a nicely-made blue roan which turned to black on his face and his legs, and he had a white mane and tail which gave him a fairy-tale quality, enhanced by his pretty rider with her coal-black locks. The judges then turned back to Nigella and the bay mare, and it was clear that they were comparing the two. Henrietta fumed, furious that Janie Richardson had turned up.

The steward waved the class on into canter. The mare-who-slipped-a-stifle cantered off smoothly, with professional ease. She was no stranger to the show ring, having been many times a champion before she had suddenly and inexplicably begun to slip her stifle out of joint. When her owners had discovered that her disability was as incurable as it was unusual, they had sold her as a brood mare, only to

41

have her returned as barren. Thus the Fanes had bought her for a song to join their stable of cut-price, slightly imperfect hirelings.

The canter sorted the class out in no uncertain manner. Some of the bolder horses began to yaw and pull, sweating up in anticipation of the gallop they knew was to come. One of them managed to get its head down in order to give three huge consecutive bucks right in front of the judge. Its rider, with any hopes of a prize dashed, asked permission to retire, and rode out through the collecting ring, her shoulders bowed with disappointment.

The mare-who-sometimes-slipped-a-stifle galloped like a dream, long and low, with strides that ate up the ground. She steadied and balanced herself beautifully on the corners, and she fairly flew down the straight, with Nigella sitting on top looking charming and aristocratic, and as cool as a cucumber. The glory of this was entirely missed by Henrietta, who kept her eyes glued to the mare's inside hindleg, as if she expected it to drop off at any moment.

To our chagrin, Summer Nights galloped just as well, and we were in an agony of apprehension as the class came back to a walk, and the judges conferred on their preliminary placings. They looked at Nigella and the-mare-who-sometimes-slipped-a-stifle for a long time, but they pulled Summer Nights in first.

Doreen let out a squawk of dismay. 'It's not fair,' she complained. 'Our horse is much nicer than that one; it looks as if it should have rockers on it.'

I could see her point. 'But the class isn't over yet,' I told her. 'The judge has to ride them and see them run up in hand.'

'If Nigella just gets the second prize,' Henrietta grumbled, 'we shall only get twenty pounds instead of fifty.' It sounded anything but sportsmanlike.

When the line had assembled, the judges asked Janie Richardson to ride out in order to give them an individual display. Summer Nights performed impeccably, trotting out with a long and level stride, striking off into canter on the right leg, and stretching out into a sweeping gallop. But when the riding judge was put up into the saddle, he became a different horse. Whether it was the extra weight he objected to, or her heavy-handed way of riding, was not altogether clear; but he completely lost all his fluent, forward-flowing movement. He trotted with an over-collected chopped stride, he cantered sideways like a crab, and when he was asked to gallop, all he could achieve was an agitated tail-swirling scuttle. Janie Richardson covered her eyes in shame and we knew that it was all over for Summer Nights.

Even though all this was to our advantage, Doreen and I felt sorry for Janie Richardson, but Henrietta was openly delighted. 'Serves her right,' she chortled, 'for coming in late.'

The bay mare, who was used to strangers clambering into her saddle, gave the riding judge a superb ride; you could tell that she was enjoying every minute, and that the uncomfortable ride she had had on the first horse only heightened her appreciation of the second. Even the in-hand display went without a hitch. It was no surprise at all when Nigella was handed the red rosette. Doreen gave a little shriek of joy, and Henrietta rubbed her hands in satisfaction. 'That's our first fifty pounds in the bag,' she said. I knew it was for the Training Fund, but it sounded terribly mercenary.

The bay mare led the winners in their lap of honour, with her polished hooves flying over the turf and the satin rosette fluttering on her bridle. When we caught up with Nigella in the collecting ring, a gentleman in a camel-hair coat was asking if she would care to name a price for the mare.

Nigella, knowing full well that the horse had never been sound for longer than a month at a time, smiled down upon him with regret. 'I'm sorry,' she said graciously, 'but I'm afraid that we could never bear to part with her.'

The gentleman, who was very taken with Nigella's beautiful face, and her hand-span waist in the old-fashioned habit, shrugged his camel-hair shoulders in good-natured resignation and patted her boot in an affectionate manner. He was glad, he was heard to remark as he walked away, that there were still people left in the world to whom money wasn't everything.

Henrietta, dressed for her class in my best two-way stretch breeches, my Weatherall tweed with the velvet collar, and my deep-pile high-crown hat, with her hair in two long plaits tied with velvet ribbons, looked extremely smart. The bad-tempered chestnut, who had looked like an advanced case of moult, had been newly clipped for the occasion; with his neatly pulled tail and his plaited mane, he resembled the ideal riding horse, but in temperament he was nothing like one.

The trouble was that the bad-tempered chestnut loathed and detested other horses. He loathed and detested them all, quite without exception, and every morning, given half a chance, he would launch himself at his stable companions with a hatred undimmed by familiarity. When we led him out of the horse-box at the show there were so many horses for him to hate all at once, that he didn't know which way to turn. He contented himself with flattening his ears, arching his neck, and grinding his teeth.

'If only he didn't have that nasty spiteful look in his eye,' Doreen moaned, 'he'd be such a pretty horse.'

The bad-tempered chestnut replied to this by letting fly with a back leg, catching Doreen on the shin.

'Ooooow!' she wailed. 'He's kicked me, the horrible thing!'

'Then you shouldn't walk behind him when I'm saddling up,' Nigella told her in a reasonable voice. 'You know what he's like.'

When we reported to the collecting ring, the show programme was running fifteen minutes late. The steward, who was looking harassed, informed us that the riding horse class would begin just as soon as the hunt had given their display.

'Oh,' said Henrietta, crossly, 'how annoying. I rather

wanted to get this over with.' The bad-tempered chestnut was being an absolute beast, hopping from foot to foot, with his chin pressed against his chest, hoping that one of the other horses would come within striking distance of his back legs so that he could get a shot at it.

'I'm beginning to wonder if this was such a bright idea after all,' said Nigella, in a voice of foreboding.

Above the crowd I caught a glimpse of scarlet. William and Forster and the huntsman were advancing across the showground with a path opening in front of them and the bitch pack at their horses' heels. When the bad-tempered chestnut saw them, he completely exploded, whether from anger or excitement one couldn't really tell. He flew backwards into the ring and began to plunge up and down in a succession of rapid *Croupade* and *Courbettes*, to the vast amusement of the ringside, some of whom applauded as Henrietta stuck gamely to the saddle with her plaits flying, rating him with some rather unladylike language.

The bitch pack flowed into the ring in a wave of lemon and white as the commentator began his introduction to their parade. 'The Midvale and Westbury hounds, one of our oldest Suffolk packs of fox-hounds, with their huntsman, Tony Welby, and their whippers-in, have kindly consented to be with us today . . .'

Henrietta, finding herself to be a reluctant participant in the parade, and looking distraught, finally raised her stick and gave the bad-tempered chestnut a mighty thwack on his ribcage. As she expected, he stopped leaping up and down and shot forward, but even Henrietta could not have foreseen what happened next.

As Forster rode past, flicking his whip to bring up a loiterer, the bad-tempered chestnut recognized a well-known adversary, whipped round before Henrietta could spot him, and planted two hind shoes firmly in the chest of Forster's grey. The grey, shocked and horrified by such unexpectedly anti-social behaviour, leapt backwards into the pack, scattering hounds left and right to a chorus of yelps and howls of anguish. He cannoned tail-on into William's cob, who rocketed forward with such velocity that William was left sitting on the grass, only yards from Forster who, precipitated over the shoulder of his grey, had landed spreadeagled like a starfish.

All this had happened within the space of half a minute and the commentator, struck all of a heap by the turn of events, could only struggle with a few disjointed sentences. '. . . Hunting the country from the coast to . . . seems to have been a mishap . . . catch the loose horses before they . . . hounds . . . seems to be the end of the . . . ' The rest was mercifully drowned by the band who manfully struck up into *If You Were The Only Girl in the World*. It seemed singularly inappropriate as Henrietta crept out of the ring leading the bad-tempered chestnut, and the huntsman galloped after William's cob, who had high-tailed it into the collecting ring, and was causing havoc amongst the assembled riding horses.

The crowd, who had relished every second of this unplanned and hair-raising pantomime, now gave its entirely sympathetic attention to Forster who, tight-lipped, and rubbing his hip, limped after his grey who in the infuriating manner of horses who suspect that they have the momentary advantage, snatched mouthfuls of grass with a cautious eye in his direction and strolled to a new patch as he approached, always managing to be fractionally out of reach.

Hounds by this time had melted away into the ring-side, and were being fed sweets and crisps and ice-cream and other forbidden things. One of them was blissfully rolling in some droppings, another sat down in the centre of the ring and scratched itself. It was not the impressive display that either the hunt or the show committee had anticipated.

Henrietta, Nigella, Doreen and myself hid ourselves away behind the members' tent until we heard the riding horses being called. We knew that not even the rousing cheer that went up as the hunt, remounted and reassembled, re-entered the ring to begin their parade afresh, would appease the fury of William and Forster and the huntsman, who knew full well that half of their subscribers had been standing at the rails to witness their embarrassment.

The bad-tempered chestnut, with all passion spent, went quite well in the riding horse class. The judges gave him some long and favourable looks, and he even managed to put his ears forward at times, such as on the approach to the two small jumps he was asked to negotiate, and during his gallop. The result of this was that Henrietta came cantering out of the ring with a yellow rosette. It may not have been the one she had wanted, but in the circumstances it was very creditable.

It was lunchtime by now, and the working hunter class was not until half past two. We despatched Doreen to fetch some' sandwiches, and Henrietta and Nigella went off with their rosettes to collect the prize-money from the secretary. I was left to lead the bad-tempered chestnut back to the horse-box.

Half way across the ground I was dismayed to see that Forster was walking towards me. He was not alone, and there was no way I could decently avoid him. I knew he would still be simply livid about the fracas with Henrietta and the bad-tempered chestnut, and I had really hoped that I woudn't have to face him until things had cooled down a bit. Yet I knew I would have to apologize for the Fanes sooner or later, and I steeled myself to get it over with. I needn't have bothered.

The other person with Forster was Janie Richardson. Forster had his arm around her. I thought he might have removed it, when he saw me, but he didn't. He just gave me an icy look and said, 'I'd have that bloody horse destroyed, if I were you.' Then Janie Richardson giggled and slipped an arm around his waist, and they walked on, looking into each other's eyes.

I felt curiously numb as I led the bad-tempered chestnut

up the ramp of the horse-box, unofficially borrowed from Thunder and Lighᴣning Limited, who had ill-advisedly left it parked in the coach-house. I rugged and bandaged the chestnut and gave him a hay net. Then I turned my attentions to Legend and my thoughts towards our appearance in the working hunter class. Or at least, I tried to; but the image of Forster with Janie Richardson kept getting in the way.

6

A Working Hunter

The pinewoods were inviting; they were dark and cool and silent, and very, very private. I would have given a lot to be able to ride away into them; to lose myself in their deepness, to ride through and beyond them, out into the brown and green and gold of bracken and gorse and tree-lupin, where the soil grew light and sandy, and dipped its pebbly fingers into the grey, unwelcoming turbulence of the North Sea.

But as I worked Legend steadily on the edge of the showground and his head gradually came down on to the bit, and he settled into his regular, fluent stride, I was cross with myself for becoming so easily depressed about Forster, when there should be other, more important things on my mind.

I told myself that there had never been anything at all serious between Forster and me, and there probably never would be. After all, he thought me a fool, he had told me as much often enough; and I worked for the Fanes whom he detested. There was also his reputation to consider. I had been warned about him times without number, so there was no earthly reason why I should get so overwrought about seeing him with Janie Richardson. Nevertheless, every time I thought about it, I felt as if I had been kicked in the stomach.

I decided not to think about it. I forced myself to put it out of my mind completely. I thought about the Training Fund and the scholarship instead, and I concentrated exclusively on schooling for the working hunter class which was due to begin in less than half an hour. Legend and I trotted faithfully in circles and serpentines, and cantered figure eights with simple changes of leg, and threw in some transitions and half-halts for good measure.

Things were going very smoothly by the time I heard the

first call for the working hunters. I rode Legend back to the horse-box, pleased by his swinging stride, his row of immaculate plaits, the eager curve of his black-tipped ears, and the silky gloss of his bay coat.

'Legend don't half look lovely,' Doreen said in a wistful voice. She held him whilst Nigella put an extra gleam to his coat and his black legs with a rubber, oiled his neat hooves, and applied vaseline highlights to his nose and round his dark, thoughtful eyes. Henrietta pulled off his tail bandage and brushed out the bottom of his straight, sleek tail exhorting me to hurry and put on my jacket. Then, with my hat brushed and my boots shining after the ministrations of Nigella's rubber, I set out for the main ring on my sponsored potential event horse, glad of the new, nut-brown double bridle we had purchased out of the Training Fund, but hoping that the stirrups wouldn't fly off the saddle.

We left Doreen walking Legend round the collecting ring whilst we walked the course. There were five fences to be jumped and they were well spread out, with lots of grass between them because, unlike a show-jumping course which has to be jumped with precision and accuracy involving much placing and collection, they were to be jumped at a good, hunting pace, not a gallop, but a fairly brisk canter.

The first jump was a plain, brush fence about three feet high, constructed of birch. 'Like the Point-to-Point fences, only smaller,' Nigella commented. The second was a log pile made of old railway sleepers stacked one on top of another to a height of about three feet six. The third was a gate with the top bar painted white.

'That needs to be jumped fairly accurately,' Henrietta said, pushing it with her foot and setting it swinging on its pins. 'It isn't fixed.'

The fourth fence was a combination which consisted of a hay rack with a rail in front of it, and an upright rustic post and rail. Nigella paced the distance and we decided that it would be three good strides between the two. I could see that I would have to be cantering fairly fast to get it right,

50

and I could also see that the post and rail was narrow and had no wings; it would be all too easy for a horse to dodge out to the side of it and Legend, although he hardly ever refused a fence, was not averse to dodging out of a difficult one, if he thought that he could get away with it. The combination fence was going to be my bogey.

The last fence was a bank made with a double row of straw bales covered with artificial grass and topped with a hog's back of silver birch poles. It was over four feet high, with a spread of about five feet six, and it was set at a crafty angle, so that after flying the combination, you had to steady up immediately in order to negotiate a hair-pin bend, then muster enough impulsion to manage the spread. It was a cleverly designed course which demanded absolute control, brain-power, and a bold horse with plenty of scope, yet to the crowd at the rails, accustomed to the thrills of the *Puissance* and the colourful fences of the show-jumping arena, it must have looked incredibly boring; five drab fences to be galloped over in the shortest possible time.

When we got back to the collecting ring, the steward was chalking up the numbers in the order of jumping which had been decided by means of a draw. He recognized Henrietta by the length of her plaits. 'The hunt is parading again at four,' he said, giving her a jovial poke in the ribs with his chalk. 'I hope you won't let us down. We're expecting it to be just as good as the last one.' Henrietta flushed at this reference to her earlier catastrophe; she was not yet ready to regard it as a joke.

I was fifth to jump which was just where I would have chosen to be. I would hate to be drawn first, because I needed to see how the other riders tackled the course, and I wouldn't want to be further down the list because of the suspense of waiting a long time to jump. As it was, Henrietta, Nigella and I stood at the rails to watch the first few. The judges were standing in the centre of the ring with their clipboards, the jump stewards took up their positions, and the first of the working hunters, a flea-bitten grey with a

51

roman nose and pink-rimmed eyes, cantered round the ring, waiting for the bell. Doreen was still walking Legend round the collecting ring.

When she heard the bell, the aged woman-rider of the grey cantered one more circle before turning into the first jump. The grey pricked his ears at the brush fence as if it was the one obstacle in the world he had been longing to jump. He cantered at it with evident enthusiasm, then suddenly changed his mind and dug in his heels at the very last moment, stopping on a violent skid, gouging two deep channels out of the turf, and landing with his pink nose on the clipped birch.

The aged woman-rider, who had shot up his neck and lost her hat, struggled back into the saddle, applied her stick to his ribs and set him back at the fence. The grey sailed over. This performance was repeated at every fence, but the pair were totally defeated by the combination, and the judges were forced to ping their bell for elimination. On the way out the grey cleared the first two fences in reverse order and without hesitation, which must have been simply infuriating for the aged woman-rider.

The next horse to jump was a little black cob with three white stockings and a blaze. He looked the sort of horse you see on chocolate boxes and calendars, but he was not the sort of horse you expected to see in a working hunter class.

'He'll be in trouble over this course,' Henrietta commented. 'He's very short-coupled and short-striding, he just doesn't have the scope.'

The little black cob sailed over the brush and the sleeper-pile in fine style, but he tipped the gate, which swung wildly and fell as he approached the combination. He cleared the hay rack, took an incredible five and a half short strides, and screwed himself up and over the rustic post and rail, dislodging the top rail with his hind legs and almost losing his rider in the process. The hair-pin bend, though, presented no problem at all, and by whipping up a certain amount of speed, his rider bustled him over the spread. The crowd gave him a round of applause for a game effort.

The third horse was a handsome chestnut gelding ridden by a determined-looking young man in a bowler hat and brown butcher boots. They cantered round the ring looking as if they meant business, and they did. They achieved a perfect round and a burst of spontaneous applause as they finished. I missed the last half of it because I was looking for Legend. When I had been ready to mount, neither he nor Doreen were anywhere to be seen in the collecting ring. They were finally found half-way across the showground, Doreen having decided to join the queue for a milkshake, and taken the horse with her. Henrietta delivered them back, Doreen by the scruff of her neck, still gripping a blue and white straw between her teeth. Nigella, displaying sound economic reasoning in the midst of high tension, said she should be allowed to go back and finish it, milk-shakes being the price they were.

'One day,' Henrietta promised, as she bolted back across the showground, 'I'll wring her skinny little neck.'

After a few cantered circles in the collecting ring, I put Legend at the practice jump. It was a thin, rustic pole balanced on two jump stands, not at all like the solid fences we had constructed in the park, and he clipped it carelessly with his heels. The second time he jumped it with inches to spare, so I left it at that and walked him over to the main ring entrance to wait our turn. The last horse to jump before us was very hot. It raced at its fences and went into the combination so fast that it couldn't even take off in time for the second part and crashed through it, taking the rails on its chest.

There was a short delay after this, whilst the judges decided whether it counted as a knock-down or a refusal, but as the horse had not actually left the ground, it was counted as a refusal, and the rider was told to jump the combination again. This time the horse managed to scrape over with one and a bit strides in between the fences, but it completely failed to negotiate the hair-pin bend and flew straight past the bank instead of jumping it. After another

53

circuit of the ring, the rider managed to steer it into the bank and the horse cleared it like a steeplechaser, and galloped past us into the collecting ring.

'Goodness,' Nigella gasped, 'it's almost as bad as The Comet.'

'It's worse,' said Henrietta. 'The Comet jumps a lot better than that; at least he doesn't flatten over his fences.'

It was my turn. Legend and I trotted into the ring to a breathless shriek of, 'Good luck, Elaine!' from Doreen, who had torn herself away from the milkshake stand and arrived in the nick of time to see Legend perform.

I had been very nervous just before the class, but now I was actually in the ring, and although I was very much aware of the crowd pressed against the rails, my nerves were steady. With the soft thud of Legend's rhythmically cantering hooves in my ears, and the supple reins of the double bridle between my fingers, I was ready and waiting for the bell, and as soon as it went I turned Legend into the first fence.

I was half-expecting him to put in one of his silly, exaggerated leaps over the birch brush, but he didn't; his ears pricked forward, his stride lengthened into it, and he jumped it perfectly. On we thudded, over the sleeper-pile, across the springy turf and into the swinging gate. We cleared it with no trouble at all. Now for the combination.

I knew I had to keep up a fairly brisk pace to get the stride right, and I also knew that the tendency is for both horse and rider to slow up instinctively when two fences loom ahead instead of one. In my anxiety to do the right thing, I pushed on too hard and I rushed Legend out of his stride. It was entirely my fault that he met the hay rack slightly wrong and took off too late and too close to the fence. He went up like a lift, both stirrups flew off the Fanes' hateful old saddle, and I crash-landed back on to it only just in time to stay with him as he put in two racing strides and soared up over the post and rails. He could so easily have run out instead, because I wouldn't have been able to do a thing about it, but

54

he carried on and took me over without so much as a look to left or the right.

I was back in balance with him in time to make the hairpin bend, and we cantered on towards the bank, lengthened into it, met it exactly right and flew over, stirrupless but triumphant, landing to the sound of applause and the shouts of the jump steward who came running with the stirrups and leathers.

The Fanes were delighted although their delight turned to agitation as six out of the fourteen horses left to jump went clear, which meant that eight of us went into the next phase of the class with similar marks.

But I didn't doubt for a moment that Legend would win the class. In the showing phase he performed as impeccably as I had known he would. He trotted and cantered and galloped and stripped better than any of the others; even the handsome chestnut gelding ridden by the young man in the brown butcher boots was well and truly outclassed. When everything goes so well, it all begins to have a dreamlike quality, and I was in a daze by the time the judges had hooked the triple-tier red rosette on to Legend's new double bridle. I almost forgot the lap of honour and followed the other prize-winners into the collecting ring. I had to be shooed back by the steward.

We cantered in front of the grandstand whilst the band played *If You Knew Susie* in quickstep tempo and the crowd did a hand-clap which turned to cheers as we gave them a spirited gallop along the rails. Legend would dearly have liked to do it again, knowing that it was really his triumph, but I brought him back to a trot as we neared the collecting ring, and rubbed his neck gratefully with my knuckles. I knew he had won the class in spite of my riding, not because of it.

There was a splash of scarlet at the ringside. It was worn by someone who stood alone at the rails beside the blackboard which still had the numbers chalked upon it. Forster didn't smile or acknowledge me at all; but our eyes locked for a brief moment before he turned and walked away.

55

The Message of the Dressage

'Working trot down centre line, at L circle to the left twenty metres diameter, X to M leg-yielding . . .' The pages of *Training the Event Horse* fairly flew, as Nigella went in pursuit of the explanation to this new mystery.

I knew all about leg-yielding, having spent hours watching Hans Gelderhol, the golden boy of eventing and three times European Champion, instructing dressage riders at the training centre where I had studied for my Horsemaster's Certificate. 'It's just a matter of the horse giving to the lateral aids and moving on four tracks,' I explained, 'it's a perfectly simple exercise.' I didn't add that I had never actually tried it.

'It doesn't sound simple to me,' Henrietta said grimly, 'it sounds jolly difficult. How on earth can any horse move along on four tracks all at once?' Henrietta hated dressage.

'There seems to be a separate track for each leg,' Nigella said, having finally come to rest at the appropriate page of her Bible. *'The horse moves along at a slight angle to the side of the arena, with his head slightly bent away from the movement, and the rider uses the lateral aids, the leg and the hand on the same side. When the horse is on four tracks,'* she read, *'one hind leg moves to a position between the forelegs, and the other moves outside the forelegs. Here, you can see how it works in this photograph.'*

Henrietta took the book with a sigh of resignation. 'I shall never understand it,' she groaned. 'I don't even see why I have to try.'

'You have to try because I need all the help I can get if I'm to stand any chance at all of winning a scholarship,' I said severely. 'I must have someone standing in front to check if Legend is actually moving on four tracks; I won't be able to tell myself. *Somebody* has to know what we're aiming for!'

We were out in the park, trying to master the sequence and the rules of the dressage test for the combined training competition. A week after Rendlesham Horse Show I had been accepted as a suitable candidate for the Hissey Training Scholarship for potential event riders, and had been sent an invitation to compete in the combined training competition to be held in three weeks' time. Three weeks should have given me ample time to prepare, but the way things were going it seemed as if I needed three years.

'This horse,' Henrietta said, squinting at the photograph, 'is amazingly like The Comet; younger of course, and smarter, and a bit more dappled, but very like The Comet all the same.'

'That's Genesis,' said Nigella, who by this time knew all the intimate details of the horses and riders pictured in *Training the Event Horse* by heart. 'He belonged to Lala Thornapple and he was one of the team when Great Britain won the Olympics. He was only six years old at the time and that's incredibly young for an Olympic horse. He was an equine infant prodigy.'

'You're not supposed to be looking at the horse anyway,' I told Henrietta impatiently, 'only noting the position of its legs to see if you can tell me when Legend is moving on four tracks.'

Henrietta gave her attention to the horse's legs and decided that she probably could.

'Then, let's start again,' I said, 'and you can stand at the end of the arena and judge the leg-yielding.'

Henrietta pulled a face but she jumped down from the rusted iron rail where she had been perched beside Nigella and went to take up her position. Our dressage arena was marked out with oil drums begged from the local garage and painted white with black letters on them. We had marked the centre X with an armful of straw and Legend had wasted the first quarter of an hour by refusing to walk across it, snorting, and running sideways and rolling his eyes. For all the fuss he made I might have been asking him to walk over an elephant trap.

'Right,' Nigella decided, 'we shall begin again.' She settled her Bible and the printed dressage sheet on her lap in order to bang a small saucepan lid with a tablespoon. This was intended to represent the bell, and it made Legend jump. I had to trot him round a few times before he could forget about it. Finally, we entered the arena.

'I'm sorry, Elaine, but you're already eliminated,' Nigella informed me. *'Any horse failing to enter the arena within sixty seconds of the bell being sounded shall be eliminated.'*

I stared at her in indignation. She was still wearing the zippered ski-pants although they were no longer the unsullied white they had been. She also wore the red pill-box with the veil pulled up lest it should impede her view of *Training the Event Horse*. Her hair was tied back with baler twine and her feet were shod with the red tap-dancing shoes. She was nobody's idea of a dressage coach.

'You might have warned me,' I complained. 'I had no idea!'

'You may begin again,' she said patiently, 'but do remember on future occasions. Now, enter at working trot, at X halt and salute . . .'

Legend and I rode wearily out of the arena and re-entered at a sitting trot, managing to achieve a level halt at X.

'Don't let him swish his tail!' Nigella cried in alarm. *'Grinding the teeth and swishing the tail are signs of nervousness or resistance on the part of the horse and will be penalized in the movement concerned and also in the collective mark at the end of the test.'*

'He isn't grinding his teeth, and he was only swishing his tail at a fly,' I said crossly. 'How can I possibly be expected to control that?'

'Also,' Nigella continued, *'the use of the voice is prohibited and will be penalized by the loss of two marks.'*

It was maddening. We would never make any progress at

all at this rate. 'They only mean you can't say things like "canter on" to the horse!' I cried in exasperation. 'We're only practising, after all!'

'I'm only telling you what it says in the book,' Nigella said in a defensive tone, 'I'm only reading out the rules.'

'And I'm beginning to see why you need professional tuition,' Henrietta said morosely from the end of the arena.

Later in the day we went on a spending spree. We went into our local saddlers and explained that we wanted to buy a really good general purpose saddle suitable for cross-country and jumping. The sales lady, who was small and grey-haired, with close-cropped hair and a leather jerkin, regarded us with interest tinged with apprehension. In the days when I had first gone to work for the Fanes, they had run up huge bills for everything connected with their livery yard, and the saddlers had been one of the creditors who had been obliged to threaten to sue. We had managed to pay them before they did, but it was hardly surprising that they should hesitate to supply us now.

'It's perfectly all right,' Nigella assured the sales lady. 'We've got the money, honestly.' She opened her bead-encrusted dorothy bag and displayed the Training Fund in the form of a wad of notes. The sales lady, reassured by this glimpse of hard cash, sped into action.

By the time I had clambered in and out of two dozen saddles, all varying in their length, shape, design and fitting, I was no longer sure what I wanted and I couldn't tell if any of them were going to fit Legend either.

'Fetch the horse,' Henrietta commanded, 'we shall have to try them on.'

Even the sales lady thought this to be an excellent idea, and in no time at all Legend was standing in the back yard amongst the jumping poles and stands, whilst the sales lady placed saddle after saddle on his back and we squinted at them from all angles. Eventually, after much agonizing and several try-out runs up and down the road involving the addition of girth and leathers and irons, we found one that suited us exactly. By the time we had paid for the saddle and some jump stands with cups and pins, we had spent almost two hundred and fifty pounds. This meant that taking into consideration the double bridle, which had cost seventy pounds, we only had fifty pounds left, and with that we had to buy a dressage saddle.

'Where on earth are we going to find a dressage saddle for fifty pounds?' I asked Nigella, as I drove the shooting brake down the road with its back bristling with jump stands, and Henrietta followed sedately behind on Legend. 'I'm sure it's going to be impossible, and there's no question of doing any more fund-raising between now and the combined training competition, there isn't time.'

'I know,' Nigella admitted. 'But I expect something will turn up. It usually does.'

And it did.

On the Monday morning after the advertisement for a saddle had appeared, we received one letter. It was written in the most hideous scrawl and signed with a totally illegible signature, but the gist of it was that the writer was the possessor of a dressage saddle which she was unable to use any more and might be willing to sell. There was no further information than this, no size or make or price, but it was the only reply we had, and we were desperate. Armed with the dorothy bag containing our last fifty pounds, we set out.

Luckily, the letter had been written on headed note-paper, so we didn't have any trouble in deciphering the address. It took us two hours to reach the small Oxfordshire village, and the house was easy to find, having two stone gateposts surmounted with rearing horses. They were a lot nicer than the Fanes' ivy-clad vulpines, one of which had toppled off its perch long ago and never been repleaced.

We drove up an immaculately maintained drive, passing a small stone-built stable yard, and parked in front of a mellow stone house with a sundial cut in above the door.

'We won't get a dressage saddle for fifty pounds from here,' Henrietta said in a depressed voice. 'People who live in houses like this always buy the very best things, they never have anything cheap.'

My heart began to lower itself down into my boots. I felt sure that she was right. We got out of the shooting brake. Through the long leaded windows of the house I could see good oak furniture, gilt framed pictures and the glint of silver on every available surface. I felt thoroughly despondent. It hardly seemed worthwhile lifting the solid brass knocker on the front door.

The door was opened by a nurse. She didn't look too welcoming. She was wearing a dark blue dress with a starched apron and black shoes and stockings. She didn't have a frilled cap. 'Yes?' she said, raising her eyebrows at us in a questioning manner. 'What do you want?'

Nigella immediately launched into a long explanation about the advertisement and the dressage saddle and the letter we had received. The nurse frowned a bit and looked disapproving, but she let us in and left us standing in a small, panelled hall. We hoped she had gone to hunt out the letter-writer.

The hall was lined with framed photographs of horses. When we looked closer we saw that they were event horses.

'Look,' Henrietta said, stabbing at one of them in astonishment. 'It's the horse in the book! It's Genesis!'

There were a lot of photographs of Genesis, performing dressage in a boarded arena, sailing over show-jumps in front of a crowd of spectators, galloping over cross-country fences.

'It can't be Lala Thornapple's house,' Nigella whispered incredulously, 'it just can't be!' But it was.

Lala Thornapple came trotting into the hall hot-foot after the nurse. She was wearing a baggy, red, track-suit with white flashes and I saw at once why her writing was so awful, her hands were crippled with arthritis. They were set in impossibly knotted positions and it made shaking hands very difficult. Lala Thornapple was old, I suppose, but her lined face was pink, and her eyes were as bright and sparkling as a child's. She seemed delighted to see us, and gave us a guided tour of the pictures, sometimes forgetting which horse was which and what they were doing at the time, which made it all rather confusing.

'What about Genesis?' Nigella asked. 'Is he still alive?'

'Alive?' Lala Thornapple threw up her gnarled hands, astonished to think that anyone could ever doubt it. 'Of course he's alive! He's out there in the stables,' she gestured through the window at the stone-built stable yard. 'They're all out there, all of these horses are in the stables; would you like to see them?'

It occurred to me that some of them must be very old by now but, 'Oh *yes*,' Nigella breathed, 'we *would*.'

'Not without a coat, Miss Thornapple,' the nurse said hastily, and whilst she was helping her charge to get her arms into an anorak, she looked at us over her shoulder and frowned and shook her head. We all looked at her blankly, not knowing what she meant.

The nurse came with us down to the stable yard looking on in resignation as Lala Thornapple chattered on and on about her horses. I thought she was probably glad to have some visitors who were interested enough to listen, because the nurse didn't look the horsey type at all.

The stable yard was beautifully kept. There was not a weed or a wisp of straw to be seen. 'You must have a jolly good groom,' Henrietta commented, 'to keep everything looking so neat and clean.'

'Oh, I have,' Miss Thornapple said happily, 'I have.'

We reached the first loose box. There was no welcoming head over the door. I felt sorry for Miss Thornapple, having horses so decrepit that they didn't fly to the door at the sound of footsteps. Nigella went to draw the bolt, but Lala Thornapple pushed her hand gently away and drew it herself, not without some difficulty, and opened the lower door. 'Now this is the famous Genesis,' she said proudly, walking into the stable and stretching out a hand to fondle his neck. 'Hello, you lovely boy, and how are you today?'

I tried not to gasp, but I couldn't help it. There was straw in the stable, beautifully bedded and laid with banked up sides, there was a water bucket filled to the brim with clean water, and there was a full hay net hung in one corner. But there was no Genesis. There was no horse at all. I looked, and I looked and I blinked, and I looked at the nurse, we all looked at the nurse, and the nurse shook her head firmly and put her finger to her lips.

'Of course,' Lala Thornapple said, 'he's quite an old boy now, aren't you my lovely? But you should have seen him in his youth, you should have ridden him. He was a flyer, you know, it took me all my time to hold him once he got going. It's the dressage you see, it develops all the muscles, it makes them very powerful, and Genesis was very good at dressage.' She patted his invisible neck and turned to us. 'Well,' she said briskly, 'let me show you the others.'

We met several more invisible horses, even managing to make admiring comments, and we listened to a recital of their successes in the early days of eventing. In the immaculate tack room there was a girl, carefully soaping an already spotless bridle.

'Ah, Carol, my dear,' Lala Thornapple exclaimed, 'and how have my darlings been today?'

The girl was obviously prepared for this. She said in a perfectly serious voice, 'Well, Dragoon's leg is very much better, the swelling has almost gone now, and Genesis has eaten up today, and they were all quite well-behaved when I rode them out this morning. Of course,' she added, giving us a totally bland look, 'the wind's dropped today, and that makes all the difference.'

'It does, my dear, it does,' Lala Thornapple agreed. She beamed at us in delight. 'You see,' she said, 'I told you I had a very good groom.'

I wondered what it would be like to be a groom to a yard full of invisible horses. How would you know which leg to bandage? How would you be able to tell if a horse had eaten up? And how on earth could you saddle up for exercise? I thought it was time to leave. Nigella obviously thought so too. She was already thanking Lala Thornapple for her kindness in showing us round as a preliminary to our departure. Henrietta was still staring at the girl groom. She looked as if she was about to say something to her, then changed her mind and turned away.

'But the saddle!' Lala Thornapple cried, throwing up her knotted hands in horror. 'You haven't seen the saddle!' She gestured anxiously at her girl groom. 'Get it down, Carol, dear, it's on the top rack, in the middle on the left-hand side.'

Carol lifted the saddle down from the rack and placed it on the saddle horse on top of a snowy white unused stable rubber. It was beautiful; soft and supple and dark brown, deep-seated with thigh rolls and a suede seat and extended girth straps. Lala Thornapple looked at it for a long time, and I fancied that her eyes glistened with tears.

'Oh, no,' I said instinctively, 'we couldn't afford it. It's perfectly lovely, it's a wonderful saddle, but it's way out of our reach.'

Lala Thornapple looked at me sharply. 'How do you know you can't afford it?' she snapped. 'I haven't told you how much it is yet.'

'Oh,' I said startled, 'I'm sorry, I only . . .'

'Don't cross her,' the nurse whispered warningly from behind my shoulder. 'Humour her if you can.' But Lala Thornapple was already beaming again.

'When I first bought this saddle,' she said, remembering, 'it was especially made for Genesis. I designed it myself and it was way ahead of its time. It isn't old fashioned you know, even now.'

'No,' Henrietta agreed warily, 'it isn't.'

'But of course it's no longer new,' Lala Thornapple said with regret, 'and although it cost all of fifty pounds to be made . . .'

'Fifty pounds!' Nigella couldn't restrain herself from exclaiming, it seemed such a paltry amount.

'It does seem a lot doesn't it?' Lala Thornapple agreed. 'But it *was* made of the finest leather and suede, and the man who made it was a master saddler. Of course, I wasn't going to ask you *anything* like that for it; what do you say to thirty pounds?' She looked at us expectantly.

'Oh,' Nigella said, aghast, 'we *couldn't!*'

'Then what about twenty-five?' Lala Thornapple said kindly.

'But that's far too cheap!' I cried. 'It's worth much, much more than that! We couldn't possibly take it!'

'You, young lady,' Lala Thornapple turned on me with her eyes shooting sparks, 'are far too stupid ever to become an event rider!' She turned her attention back to Nigella.

'Take it,' the nurse muttered behind my shoulder. 'Go on, tell her you'll take it. She'll be ever so upset if you don't, and I'll have to cope with her afterwards. Money means nothing to her, and she's had a lovely time showing you the horses. She'll relive all this for months.'

So we took the saddle, Genesis' saddle, handmade from the finest leather and suede by a master craftsman, for the princely sum of thirty pounds. We were not proud of our bargain. We walked away from the immaculate yard peopled by ghosts and memories, leaving Lala Thornapple standing beside her nurse, waving her ruined hands; hands that had once guided a horse through an Olympic dressage test, and calling out to us that she might even come to watch the two-day event just for old time's sake.

Nobody said much on the way home. Only Nigella spoke, staring fixedly ahead into the twin pools of the headlights on the road. 'When we're rich,' she said, 'and we can afford another dressage saddle, we'll take this one back and we'll leave it, just as it was, on the top rack, in the middle, on the left-hand side.'

8

All in the Mind

'There seem to be an awful lot of horses and riders here,' Nigella commented as we bumped on to the ground where the combined training competition was to be held. 'They can't *all* be scholarship candidates.'

'I expect some of them have just been invited to make up the numbers,' Henrietta said, 'to make it more of a competition.'

I took no part in this conversation because I wasn't feeling well and it was taking me all my time to steer the horse-box. I had hardly slept a wink last night, I had just tossed and turned and worried ceaselessly about the dressage. I just knew that the test was going to be a disaster.

'They all look very professional, don't they?' Nigella said admiringly, as we turned into a parking space at the end of a line of smart horse-boxes. 'You can tell it isn't just a horse show, all the horses are really expensive top quality animals.'

'But then,' Henrietta pointed out, 'so is Legend.' She glanced at me as if to suggest it was the rider who might prove less than satisfactory.

'I think I'm going to be sick,' I said.

'Rubbish,' Henrietta countered in an unsympathetic voice. 'It's all in your mind. Don't be so feeble.'

As I parked the horse-box, the people next door gave us covert sideways glances. It wasn't, for once, because we looked so awful. Rather the reverse was true. The horse-box had been custom-built for our livery clients with gleaming black coachwork and a red trim. There was a Rolls Royce insignia on its bonnet. The sordid truth of the matter was that a hired box would have cost us fifty pounds and we couldn't have afforded it. As it was, after we had paid twelve pounds to have our unsuspecting pop group's petrol tank filled up, all we had left of the Training Fund in Nigella's bead-encrusted dorothy bag were eight single pound notes.

The Fanes jumped down from the cab and looked round with appreciation. The combined training ground was a magnificent sweep of sheep-nibbled turf. In the May sunshine the white boards of the dressage arena were brilliant against the emerald turf, and the show-jumps in their roped-off ring were a dazzle of red and blue and white. There was a small secretary's tent and some trestle tables set under a tree where ladies were already laying out cakes, sandwiches and paper cups for coffee and soft drinks. It was a lovely rural English scene, with even a Jacobean mansion away in the distance, but the sight of it all made me feel sicker than ever.

'I'll go and fetch the numbers, ' Nigella offered, 'and the dressage timings. I expect they will be ready by now.' She skipped off across the grass in her zippered ski-pants, newly laundered for the occasion. She had never been to a combined training competition before but already she knew the form; *Training the Event Horse* had taught her all she knew.

Doreen was at school, the combined training being on a weekday, so we were without her dubious services as messenger and groom. Henrietta and I got Legend unboxed and took off his rugs and bandages. He was sweating slightly and I realized that I had over-rugged him, unaccustomed as I was to such luxurious draught-proof transport. I tottered around him with a rubber, drying off his wet patches and feeling absolutely dreadful. I didn't know where I was going to find the strength to mount, let alone ride a dressage test. I had never had such an appalling attack of nerves in my life and I was at a loss to understand it. Henrietta, observing that I was totally useless, tacked up. The dressage saddle had fitted Legend perfectly. The sight of it should have given me confidence, but it didn't.

I sat on the ramp and tried to read through the test. I was sure that I was going to lose my way.

A Enter at working trot (sitting)
X Halt. Salute
Proceed at working trot (sitting)
C Track Left
E Circle Left 20m diameter . . .

Far from being familiar, it was as if I had never seen it before in my life, and when I got to the complicated bit with the circle off the centre line and the leg-yielding, the print started to move in front of my eyes.

Nigella came back. She handed me a number and a typed list of dressage timings. The tests were timed at seven minute intervals throughout the morning, leaving the afternoon free for the show-jumping. Mine was the eleventh test on the list, timed for 11.10A.M., and there were thirty-one tests altogether.

'They're all scholarship candidates,' Nigella informed me, 'and they short-list twelve – I asked.'

'You really must mount, Elaine,' Henrietta said anxiously. 'You have to do your schooling, then come back to smarten up, there isn't much time.'

'And according to the rules,' Nigella added, 'you need to be riding in close to the arena twenty minutes before your starting time.'

I tried to pull myself together. The first horse was already performing his test inside the white boards; in just over an hour I would be performing mine. I put on my hat.

'You'll be perfectly all right once you start schooling,' Nigella said reassuringly, 'honestly you will.'

I hoped she was right. I checked Legend's girth and mounted, tucking the dressage test sheet into the pocket of the jeans I was wearing to protect my good breeches. Legend felt very alert and bouncy as I rode away from the horse-box to find a quiet place to school. The dressage saddle gave me a far greater area of contact and a vastly improved 'feel'; it was easy to imagine that I was actually part of Legend, not merely a passenger giving directions from on top.

68

I began to work Legend in around a majestic oak tree. He felt much fitter and livelier than usual and I made a mental note to tell Nigella to cut down his corn. It took longer than usual to get him to concentrate and to relax, but finally we got into our stride and I began to feel slightly better. My head was muzzy and my throat was dry, but the test had come back to me and I felt there was a sporting chance I might get through it without losing my way. In no time at all three-quarters of an hour had gone by and it was time to go and get ready.

Nigella had fetched coffee for us and I drank mine down gratefully to lubricate my throat. I put on my navy jacket and brushed up my hat, but when I leaned over to buff up my boots, my head felt as if it was going to fall off. I stood up and leaned against the side of the horse-box, agonized.

'Do come on, Elaine!' Henrietta called impatiently. She had sponged Legend's bit and oiled his hooves and pulled off his tail bandage. Nigella was giving him a last minute polish with a rubber. I tied on my number; it was thirteen. I felt awful again. If I was going to feel like this every time I had to ride a dressage test, I didn't think I would be able to stand it; my nerves would never last out. I would be a mental wreck. Perhaps Lala Thornapple was right after all and I was far too stupid ever to become an event rider.

'What happens if I ride a terrible test? What happens if we don't get short-listed for the scholarship?' I asked the Fanes. 'What happens then?'

'We'll cross that bridge when we come to it,' Nigella said firmly. She steadied the off-side stirrup whilst I struggled into the saddle. Legend rolled his eyes and pranced a bit. 'He's having too much corn,' I said, 'he's too lively.'

'Rubbish,' Henrietta said crossly, 'it's just because he hasn't had enough prep. Honestly, Elaine, I don't know what's got into you, you're being *hopeless*. Anybody would think you didn't want the scholarship!'

'I do,' I muttered, 'I've got stage-fright, that's all.'

We made our way across to the dressage arena and

69

watched one of the horses perform its test from the ropes which kept everyone twenty yards from the boards so that other horses should not affect the concentration of the one being judged. 'Look,' Henrietta said in delight, 'he's having terrible trouble with his leg-yielding, he can't do it at all. He won't get any marks for that!'

Slightly heartened to see someone else making heavy weather of the dressage, I took Legend off to ride him in within sight of the steward who was in charge of the starting order. The judge was sitting with her writer in a Range Rover opposite the centre line at the C end of the arena and they gave the signal to start by a blast on the hooter.

If anything, this was more unnerving than the spoon and saucepan lid, and I worked Legend as close as I could get to the vehicle, hoping that by the time our turn came he would be used to it. The tests were running ten minutes late and I was glad of the extra time.

When my number was finally called Legend had settled and resigned himself to the idea of work. I knew that once he had reached this stage he would be very consistent, not easily shaken out of his stride, and very obedient; he might not be experienced nor very skilled at dressage, but he would try for me, and that was all I wanted.

We were allowed two minutes inside the boards to accustom ourselves to working in the arena before starting the test. This was a blessing because Legend didn't like the sparkling boards and leaned away from them, rolling his eyes. If this had happened during the test it would have lost us valuable marks. As it was, he soon got over it and we trotted out of the arena and waited at the top, just behind A. My hands felt clammy on the reins, my eyes felt hot, but I had nerved myself to the test and I was fully in control. The Range Rover sounded its hooter, this was it.

A Enter at working trot (sitting)
H Halt. Salute . . .

My nerves, my muzzy head, my dry throat, everything was

70

forgotten in the solid concentration of trying to perform a good test. My world was reduced to the plaited neck and the pricked ears in front of me and the level thud of hooves below; contained within the white boards with their black letters; and directed by the printed sheet of the dressage test. Nothing else mattered. Nothing else existed.

Circle Left 20m diameter. I noticed that Legend bent his neck, rather than his whole body. My fault that, not enough leg, must do better next time. *K-M working canter*, on the right leg, thank goodness, but don't look down to see. *Sitting trot, A Halt, immobile 4 seconds,* moved off a fraction too smartly there due to Legend's over-anticipation. *K-M Change the rein at working trot,* turn up centre line, *circle 20 metres,* a better bend this time. *Leg-yielding*, started off all right degenerated into crab-wise trot, still, that's one over. Working trot, canter, turn down centre line, last of the leg-yielding; this time it's half-pass by accident, but at least we're trying. *D working trot (sitting) G Halt, Salute. Leave arena at A at free walk on a long rein.*

It was over. I rode across to the Fanes feeling weak and light-headed. I could hardly believe that I had got through it. It may not have been a well-executed test, but we had done our best; we had tried.

Henrietta slapped Legend on his neck as I rolled out of the saddle. 'It was a jolly good effort,' she said, pleased, 'considering everything.'

'We'll go and put Legend away, then we'll come back and wait for the results to be posted,' Nigella said. She was flushed and excited, sure that we had done well.

We stood by the score boards, waiting for my marks to be posted up. Nobody seemed to have done very well. Most of the marks were up in the hundreds. Somebody remarked in a disgruntled voice that it had been a ridiculously difficult test for novice horses to perform; scholarship trial or no scholarship trial.

The method of scoring was very complicated. There were 140 marks which could be awarded for the whole test, the test being divided into movements for which the judge awarded marks out ot ten, the total of marks were added, the penalty points deducted, and the resulting figure deducted from 140. Thus the lower the score, the better the test.

When my score came up it was 81. It wasn't a good score as dressage scores go, but it was good enough to put me in the lead. Henrietta and Nigella almost stood on their heads with delight. I went cold and then hot, thought I was going to faint; then bolted for the ladies' and heaved my heart up.

9

Too Awful to Contemplate

'The jumping's going to be nothing after the dressage,' Henrietta said in a confident tone. 'Absolutely nothing.'

'The fences are easy,' Nigella said, 'look at them. The highest is only three feet six inches, and they're jolly well spread out, it isn't like a proper show-jumping course at all.'

'It's just the combination fence you will have to watch,' Henrietta warned. 'Be sure you don't let Legend run out; you know he'll try if he thinks he has a sporting chance of getting away with it.'

Legend and I were standing in the collecting ring waiting our turn to jump. My stomach was churning and I could see spots dancing in front of my eyes. At the end of the dressage tests I had lost my lead and dropped to third place. It was still better than any of us had expected. Now I had to get through the show-jumping. We had walked the course and the Fanes were right when they said it was not a difficult course; the only fences that presented any problems at all were the triple combination and the water jump. We were jumping in reverse result order and I was third from the last to jump. There had been a lot of clear rounds, the scholarship candidates seemed to be a lot better at show-jumping than they were at dressage. It was all very nerve-racking, and right at the last moment I had to shoot off to the ladies' again, clambering back into the saddle just as the horse in fourth place completed the fourteenth clear round. I rode into the ring feeling very shaky, knowing that I had to get a clear round. Anything less would be a disaster.

I cantered Legend in a circle, listening for the bell. Either he was feeling a bit strong, or I was losing my grip completely; but it took me all my time to hold him going into the first fence. He flew over it, far too fast, and I heard his hind legs brush through the birch. I managed to steady him in time for the next fence, a Road Closed, and the fence after that, which was parallel poles. He was going on too strongly for the upright gate, but by putting in a big jump, he managed to clear it. I felt myself loosen in the saddle, but I pushed him on towards the water at a fair gallop, wanting to be sure he would make the spread and not wanting to give him much time to think about it. It was the first time we had ever jumped water. To do him credit, Legend didn't even hesitate; he took a flying leap and landed with yards to spare. By this time my arms felt like lead and I had to summon every last ounce of strength I had in my body to bring him back to a manageable canter. His neck felt like a piece of tensile steel, then, at the approach to the stone wall, he took me completely by surprise and put in one of his hateful, monumental bucks.

When the Fanes had first bought Legend, he had bucked me off lots of times; he had even bucked me off the first time I had ever ridden him. Gradually though, as I had learned to sit on and give him a wallop, instead of flying over his head, he had begun to desist, and now he rarely bucked. Today, he had clearly had enough of my feeble behaviour and he wanted to get rid of me. It was a miracle that I didn't fall off there and then, but I didn't. I managed to cling on and push him into the next fence and I was still hanging there by the skin of my teeth as we went, hopelessly fast, into the triple combination. I lost one stirrup over the first part, the other over the second, and when he ran out of the third part I fell over his dropped shoulder and landed in a little group of conifers.

For the rest of my life I shall never forget how it felt to pick myself up out of the broken flower-pots and flattened greenery as Legend flew round and round the ring at an enthusiastic gallop, looking mightily pleased about the whole affair. I had incurred three penalty points for a disobedience, eight for a fall, and every second spent stumbling after Legend was costing me another two penalty points for exceeding the time allowed.

By the time the ring steward had captured Legend and I

had remounted, I was numb with despair. Anger was not far behind. It was anger that gave me the strength I needed to leg Legend into the combination again, get him over it without running out, and to finish the course. It was only when I reached the collecting ring that I noticed my left wrist had blown up like a balloon and that my hand was virtually useless. To cap all the other misfortunes, I had sprained my wrist.

'You can't possibly drive home with only one arm,' Nigella said. 'I shall have to drive the horse-box.'

I knew she hadn't a driving licence, but I was almost beyond caring. Henrietta and I had had a blazing row and we were hardly speaking to one another. She seemed to think that I had thrown away all our chances on purpose. 'You knew you had to watch him at the triple,' she had raged. 'You just let him run out! You didn't lift a finger to stop him!'

'I couldn't,' I had said. 'Once he got going he was too strong. He bucked, he's too fresh, I told you, he's having too much corn.'

'That's right,' Henrietta had shrieked. 'Now it's our fault. Go on, blame us, we don't care!'

Nigella had been forced to intervene with calming words and now she was having to drive the horse-box home without a licence. If we had a crash, I knew whose fault it would be. I sat slumped against the door of the cab, feeling like hell. I had just about managed to live through what would quite possibly turn out to be the worst day of my life, and stretching ahead was a lifetime of penny-pinching and fund-raising too awful to contemplate. I just wanted to die.

But worse was to come. As we waited at the gateway of the combined training ground for permission to pull out on to the road, the officer in charge of directing the traffic walked across to us. His face looked grim.

'Oh no,' Henrietta groaned, 'he's all we need!'

The officer walked up to Nigella's open window.

'All right, young lady,' he said in a threatening voice. 'Where's your tax disc?'

Nigella stared at him, appalled. 'I don't know,' she said, 'maybe it's fallen off the windscreen.'

Henrietta got down on her hands and knees in the cab, pretending to have a look.

'You do have a tax disc?' he demanded, in a tone which implied that he knew perfectly well we hadn't.

'Yes . . . well, as far as I know we do . . .' Nigella faltered, unsure of her ground. 'You see I don't . . . I mean, it isn't . . .'

'It isn't what, miss?' the officer said, staring at her with studied patience.

'What I mean to say,' said Nigella, 'is that it isn't really our vehicle.'

The officer immediately took out his notebook and wrote down the registration number of the horse-box. 'It wouldn't be a stolen vehicle, would it, miss?' he said in an expressionless voice.

At this, Henrietta sprang up from the floor of the cab. 'It certainly is *not* stolen,' she said in an annoyed tone. 'It's borrowed from some very good friends of ours! How dare you even suggest it!'

'Now then, miss,' the officer said sternly, 'there's no need to lose your temper.' He turned back to Nigella. 'I shall have to see your driving licence, if you wouldn't mind.'

'She hasn't got it with her,' Henrietta said smartly. 'It's at home.'

'I didn't expect to be driving,' Nigella confessed truthfully. 'Our driver got bumped in the show-jumping,' she waved an arm vaguely in my direction, 'Elaine usually drives.'

'And is the vehicle insured for you to drive, miss?' the officer enquired. 'It *is* insured, I trust?'

'Of course it's insured,' Henrietta snapped. She knew perfectly well that it wasn't; that Thunder and Lightning Limited only ever insured it for the hunting season.

I really couldn't stand any more of this. I lay back in my seat and closed my eyes, overcome by giddiness, and wondering if there was room for me to pass out. I could see us all in court for driving a vehicle without a licence while it was not taxed and insured, and furthermore, I could see us losing our best livery clients, whose regular weekly cheques carried us through the winter. If we lost them we would be entirely ruined. Legend would have to be sold and I would be out of a job. I should have to go home to my father and being again, searching through the Situations Vacant in *Horse and Hound*. It was altogether more than flesh and blood could stand. I let out a loud groan at the thought of it. The officer put his face to the windscreen and stared at me through the glass.

'She's broken her arm,' Henrietta lied, 'and quite possibly sustained internal injuries as well. We're taking her to hospital.'

The officer's expression changed from one of alarm to one of fury. 'Then why the bloody hell didn't you say so in the first place?' he demanded angrily. Hs stepped back into the traffic and waved us on furiously, anxious not to delay us a moment longer in case he was left with a corpse on his hands.

I must have looked almost as bad as I felt.

10

Where are the Horses?

'We weren't quite fair,' Henrietta said, 'we didn't realize you were really ill; we thought it was just nerves.' She sat down on the faded tapestry bedcover.

'And we agree with you about the corn,' Nigella said, 'Legend *is* over the top. We've had to cut his ration by half, he's bucked us both off; Henrietta twice.' She looked at me, shamefaced.

I wasn't going to say I told you so. I sighed and gave them a weak smile intead. I had been in bed for a week battling with a particularly virulent dose of 'flu. I was in no real hurry to get better; there didn't seem much to get better for.

'We've bought you a present,' Nigella said. She laid a brown paper package on the bedclothes, where I could reach it. 'We hope you like it.'

'In fact,' Henrietta said, recovering some of her spirit and looking smug, 'we know you will.'

In spite of myself, I was touched by this unexpected show of concern and generosity. 'You shouldn't have,' I told them, 'you can't afford it.'

'Oh, it didn't cost a lot,' Nigella said, 'at least, not compared with what it's actually worth.'

I pulled myself up on to one elbow in order to investigate the bargain. I peeled off the paper. Underneath was a navy blue guernsey sweater. Mine.

'But it's my own sweater,' I said, 'my guernsey!'

'We thought you would be rather pleased to have it back,' Nigella said, 'so we spent the last of the Training Fund to redeem it. We thought you deserved it.'

At the mention of the Training Fund, any pleasure I had felt in seeing my good guernsey again immediately evaporated.

'We won't be needing the Training Fund any more,' Henrietta went on, 'not since we've had this.' She handed me an envelope. It was addressed to me, but the Fanes had opened it nevertheless. I was too weary to make a fuss. I pulled out the piece of paper it contained and opened it out. It was headed *The Hissey Training Scholarship for Potential Event Riders*, and the message was brief and to the point.

> The examiners are pleased to inform you
> that you have been short-listed for the
> above, and are hereby invited to further
> participate in a two-day event on June 20th,
> the details of which are enclosed separately.

I simply couldn't believe it. I read it over and over again. 'We've done it!' I shrieked, 'we're on the short-list!' I jumped up in bed, and reeled back against the pillows as my head started to thump and the Fanes blurred in front of my eyes.

'Yes,' Nigella said in a pleased voice. 'You are. But then,' she added, 'I always knew you would be.'

'But I can't understand why,' I said, 'when there were so many others who did better!'

'The dressage was obviously more important than we thought,' Henrietta said. 'And, after all, it was potential they were judging, not necessarily performance, they obviously believe you both could do very much better, with the professional training and everything.'

'So if you would care to recover,' Nigella said, 'we can start training for the two-day event.'

With only a fortnight before the two-day event, there was no time to waste. Two days later I was out in the yard, and the day after that I got back on Legend and took him out to do some road work. My wrist wasn't up to anything more ambitious yet, but the swelling had gone down, and strapped up by Nigella in a crepe tail bandage, it felt comfortable and I was able to use my hand within reason.

Legend and I trotted along the quiet lanes between wide acres of ripening corn. The banks and verges were thick with primroses and the countryside looked fresh and green. Now and then we passed an isolated pink-washed timber-framed cottage with a couple of terriers yapping at the garden gate, or a fat cat asleep on the window-ledge. It was all very lovely and peaceful; even the inevitable wind was tamed today, reduced to a fresh breeze which made pleasant what might otherwise have been a day too hot for riding.

I rode along feeling pleased with everything. We had been very lucky so far. We had been lucky at the Point-to-Point, lucky at the horse show, and as it had turned out, even lucky at the combined training competition. I saw no reason why the same luck should not carry us through the two-day event. If it did, Legend and I would have at least a foot in the door of the eventing world. It would be marvellous. Lost in satisfactory thoughts such as this, Legend and I turned off the lane into the bridleway that meandered round the back of the kennels. We didn't see Forster until we almost fell over him.

'Hello, Elaine,' he grinned up at me, 'imagine seeing you!'

'Yes,' I said coolly, 'imagine.' I wouldn't have stopped for anything, but before I could ride on by, he had caught Legend by the rein.

I stared at him angrily, my idyllic ride rudely interrupted. I had almost forgotten Forster in the last few weeks and I didn't want to be reminded now. 'Let go of my rein,' I said. 'I'm busy.'

'You don't look very busy,' he replied, 'you look as if you're having a nice, relaxing ride. I like your hair loose like that, it looks very pretty.' He smiled at me, all white teeth and black hair and blue eyes and suntan. He was wearing jeans and an open-necked shirt with a heavy silver chain around his neck. I could happily have throttled him with it.

'What are you doing here anyway,' I demanded indignantly, 'lurking in the bushes and jumping out on people Anyone would think you were a Peeping Tom.'

'I'm not lurking in the bushes or jumping out on people at all,' he said. 'I've just been re-hanging a gate. It's called summer maintenance, it's part of my job.'

I looked at the gate behind him and saw that this was clearly true.

'So, you're on the short-list,' he commented. He let go of Legend's rein, but he didn't move any further away.

'Yes,' I said, surprised. 'How did you know?'

'You forget,' Forster said, 'I know Felix Hissey quite well. I'll probably be with him at the two-day event. Perhaps I'll be allowed to buy you a drink?'

'You and me and Janie Richardson?' I said. 'Wouldn't three be rather a crowd?'

He grinned.

'Well,' I said crossly, 'wouldn't it?'

'I do believe you're jealous,' he said.

I denied it.

'You can come out with me tonight, if you like,' he said. 'I could pick you up at eight.' He made it sound as if he would be doing me a favour.

'No thanks,' I said. 'Ask Janie Richardson.'

'I already have,' he said. 'I'm picking her up at seven-thirty.'

'*Oh!*' I said, infuriated, 'you *pig!*' I swung my foot at him angrily, Forster grabbed my ankle and pulled me out of the saddle. Legend walked off up the bridleway. I went to run after him but Forster pulled me back, pinned me against the gate, and clamped his mouth over mine. Then, before I had time to recover my senses, he was strolling off across the field towards the white-washed buildings of the kennels with his hands in his pockets.

All this left me speechless. I picked up the nearest chunk of baked clay and hurled it after him. I'm not usually a good shot, but it hit him squarely on the back of his head. I didn't wait to see what would happen next. I ran down the bridleway to capture Legend, feeling that at least I'd made my point.

Later in the day, I was sitting on the tack room table staring at a photograph in *Training the Event Horse.* The photograph showed Genesis, in his handmade saddle, performing a half-pass at the Olympic Games. I looked at the grey horse carefully, pondering the angles of his head, the set of his neck, and the shape of his powerful, dappled hindquarters. Lala Thornapple must have been about forty-five when the photograph had been taken. She still looked young and slim and completely in unison with the horse; her legs firmly against his sides, and the reins running through her skilled, strong fingers.

Doreen came whistling into the yard on her bicycle to begin her evening stint, setting fair the stables for the horses who were still brought in at night. I hadn't realized it was so late. I put down the book and went to help. There were only three horses to bring in.

Legend was one, and The Comet, and Nelson. The last two were utilized as company for Legend when he was doing roadwork, and as transport and grandstand seats for the Fanes when we were schooling over the jumps and cross-country fences in the park.

I had collected the headcollars and was on my way out of the yard, when Henrietta appeared in a striped apron to tell me I was wanted on the telephone. 'He wouldn't say who he was,' she said in a disapproving tone, 'but if you ask me, it's Nick Forster.'

I walked back across the yard and called to Doreen to bring the horses in from the park.

'Don't let Doreen bring them up,' Henrietta objected, 'you know what a fool she is, she'll never be able to catch them.'

'Ow,' Doreen squawked, indignantly, 'I will then!'

'All the same,' Henrietta said despondently, as Doreen went off hung with headcollars and armed with a corn scoop, 'I bet she won't.'

I followed Henrietta into the kitchen. It was full of steam. Lady Jennifer was leaning over a bubbling jam kettle on the

Aga, staring at the contents in anguish. Nigella was topping and tailing gooseberries in the sink. Lady Jennifer's latest project was a produce stall in the local market square in aid of the Red Cross. The Red Cross jam didn't appear to be doing very well; little saucers with drips of brown liquid on them were dotted all over the kitchen.

'I'm having the most *ghastly* time with this batch, Elaine,' Lady Jennifer sighed, 'it's an *appallingly* bad set, and it's been boiling for hours; it's *frightfully* concentrated, and the most *revolting* colour.' It also smelled burned, but I hadn't the heart to say so. I went into the office and picked up the telephone receiver.

'Elaine,' Forster's voice said, 'I've got a lump on the back of my head the size of a grapefruit, and I'm thinking I might sue.'

'Do,' I said, 'and I'll sue as well, possibly for assault.'

Henrietta who had followed me into the office, looked up, startled.

'I'm not really all that interested in Janie Richardson,' Forster said, 'she's doing all the chasing, not me.'

'But you are taking her out tonight,' I said. 'It wasn't a joke, was it?'

He didn't deny it.

'Look,' I said impatiently, 'what do you want? It isn't very convenient to talk at the moment; I'm just about to fetch the horses in.' I rather wished Henrietta would go away, but neither of the Fane sisters had any qualms about opening other people's letters or listening in to their private conversations.

'Since you ask so nicely,' Forster said, 'I want to ask if you'll come out for a drink on Friday night.'

A germ of an idea began to take shape inside my head. I still had to get even with Forster. I didn't want to sound too keen. 'I might,' I said, in a non-committal sort of way, 'I'll think about it.'

'Think about it now,' he said, 'I want to know.'

'All right,' I said, 'I will.'

'I'll call for you at eight,' Forster said.

'Will there be two of us?' I enquired, 'or three?'

The line went dead.

'Do taste this, Elaine,' Lady Jennifer said. She looked hot and bothered with her hair escaping from a scarf and blobs of jam all over her blouse, which meant it had to be washed again; it had already been laundered so many times that it was impossible to tell what its original colour had been. Henrietta and Nigella were now arranging jam jars in lines on the kitchen table.

'Would you like to go out on Friday night?' I asked them. 'I've been asked out by Nick Forster, and I thought it might be rather jolly if we all went.'

'What a simply *marvellous* idea,' Lady Jennifer trilled. 'It will be *infinitely* more fun, and so *very* sensible to go out in a crowd instead of a twosome; how *terribly* nice of you to suggest it, Elaine.' She held out the jam spoon in an encouraging manner.

'Hrmm,' Henrietta said suspiciously. She licked her fingers and grimaced at the taste. 'Does Forster know? Would he mind?' As she had been listening to our telephone conversation she knew perfectly well that he didn't know, and that he would mind very much indeed.

'Why should he mind?' I said innocently.

Henrietta gave me a conspiratorial grin.

'We'd love to come,' Nigella said, 'if you're quite sure we won't be in the way; we've had enough of gooseberries, one way or another.'

I tasted the jam.

'I think you've forgotten to put the sugar in it,' I said.

Outside in the yard I expected to see three heads hanging over the stable doors in anticipation of the evening feed. There were none. I sighed as I realized that Henrietta had been proved right and Doreen hadn't been able to catch the horses. I had provided myself with a spare headcollar and half a bucket of corn, when I heard galloping hooves on the drive. Almost at once, Nelson appeared under the clock arch, scrabbling his boxy feet on the cobbles in a desperate effort to keep himself upright, and there was Doreen clinging to his mane with her eyes panic-stricken and her face like chalk.

'The horses,' she screeched, 'we've got to save the horses!' She yanked at the headcollar rope in the nick of time to prevent herself from being decapitated as Nelson made for the safety of his stable.

'What on earth do you mean?' I shouted at her. 'Where are the horses?'

'They all pushed out of the gate when I was getting on Nelson!' she shrieked. 'It wasn't my fault, Elaine. *Honest!*' She struggled wildly with the one-eyed bay, pulling his nose round to her boot, flailing at his ribs, and setting him in motion like a demented spinning top. 'They've all galloped away down the road! All of them have gone, your Legend and The Comet, and the chestnut and the bay mare, and they'll all be run over by cars and break all their legs, and *oh!* Henrietta Fane's going to *kill* me!' At this her voice rose to such a bawl of hysteria that it brought the Fanes tumbling out of the kitchen door, still clutching their sugar packets.

I ran for the shooting brake.

85

11
Luck of a Kind

The park gate leaning open and the headcollars strewn across the drive bore witness to the flight of the horses.

'Stop! We must look in the park!' Nigella cried, 'they may have come back!'

'Never!' Henrietta shouted. 'They wouldn't come back! Go on, Elaine! Go *on*!'

I dithered helplessly at the end of the drive, not knowing which way to go.

'Left!' Henrietta commanded.

'No,' Nigella shrieked, 'right, look! There are hoof-marks on the verge!'

We bucketed along the lane, looking fruitlessly in gateways and across the fields of corn, our eyes raking the landscape for any sight of the horses, our ears alert for any sound that might give a clue to their whereabouts. Doreen took no part in this, she just leaned her head in the bucket of corn and wept and whimpered on about cars and broken legs, and was no use to anyone; yet she had refused to stay behind, and Lady Jennifer had been left to cope with Nelson, whilst the Red Cross jam boiled away unattended on the Aga.

With my nose practically resting on the windscreen I followed the hoof marks on the verge and the half-moon bruise marks on the tarmac. I didn't dare to think too much about what we were going to find along the way. I knew that apart from a seasonal policy to cover our hunter liveries and the people who rode our hirelings, we had no insurance whatsoever, and that the consequences of any accident, both in loss or damage to the horses, or in compensation claims from any other parties involved, could be catastrophic.

Henrietta and Nigella bounced up and down on the back

seat in a fever of anxiety and impatience which grew even more frenzied as we neared the main road.

'If they've strayed on to the A12,' Nigella moaned, clasping her hands over the back of my seat in an attitude of prayer, 'God help us all!'

Doreen's wails increased in crescendo. Henrietta reached out and cuffed her into a silence broken only by an occasional strangled sob into the bucket. The hoof-prints led us to the junction where the lane met the main road. As I indicated to turn out on to the dual-carriageway, first to the left then to the right, in a welter of indecision, two things happened. The first was that the horses passed by. Led by The Comet they galloped across our vision with their necks stretched and their tails streaming and their hooves ringing out on the road. They looked neither to the left nor to the right, driven on like wild horses in a stampede by a line of nose-to-tail traffic following remorselessly on their heels.

The second thing that happened was that I stalled the shooting brake. The hand-brake didn't work due to Lady Jennifer's habit of driving round with it on, and as we slipped backwards down the incline, gathering speed, the Fanes screamed, Doreen upset the corn, and all was pandemonium. After a succession of bucks and leaps I managed to set the shooting brake lurching forward again. This time we shot straight across to the central reservation and narrowly avoided being cut in half by a Jaguar.

'Oh goodness, Elaine,' Nigella gasped, 'are you going to kill us all?' The tone of her voice suggested it might be the best way out of a nasty situation.

The pile-up of traffic behind the horses would not let us overtake. We scuttled hysterically in its wake, being hooted at by cars and sworn at by lorry drivers, and all the time we sounded our horn and flashed our lights, waving our head-collars out of the windows and crying uselessly that we were trying to catch the horses. Then the traffic suddenly started to speed up.

'The horses must have turned off!' Nigella cried, but by

87

this time we were stuck fast in the middle lane, carried helpless as a stick in a stream, past the turning where the wide grassy verges bore the unmistakable dent of horses' hooves.

'Turn back! Turn back!' Henrietta screamed, but she could see it was hopeless. It was several miles before we reached a roundabout and sped back the way we had come, fretting and lamenting on the central reservation whilst we waited for the oncoming traffic to allow us to cross.

There was no traffic at all on the side road. We hurtled along with our eyes on the verges and it was only by sheer chance that Henrietta looked up and saw that the stampede was now coming in our direction.

'The brakes!' she shouted. 'Elaine! Put on the brakes!'

With The Comet still in the lead, the horses crashed towards us up the lane. I jammed my foot on the brake and we all flew forward, only the bucket saved Doreen from being pitched on to the windscreen. The shooting brake skidded across the road. Nigella, who had opened the door and jumped out before it had stopped, vanished from sight with a horrified shriek. She reappeared, still shrieking, holding out her arms in the face of the stampede.

The Comet, observing that his route was blocked, hesitated in his stride. His gallop became a canter and his canter became a trot. Then, in his own infuriatingly cool manner, he stopped on the verge and studied the distant pinewoods with profound interest, as if the skidding hooves behind were nothing to do with him at all.

We had actually got the headcollar on The Comet and the black horse, and everything might then have been all right, but for the car which came flying round the bend. To be fair to the driver, he hardly expected the lane to be full of horses, and there was no way, brake as he might, he could have avoided hitting one of them, slamming into its side and bowling it over on the tarmac. It seemed mightily unfortunate though, that the horse he hit was Legend.

The next hour was a horrific blur. I remember Legend

struggling to get back on his feet with his flank torn open and his blood spreading in an ever-widening pool. I remember Doreen's screams and the terror in the face of the driver who shook and shook until his teeth chattered. I remember Henrietta racing along the lane like a maniac to find the nearest house with a telephone so she could summon the vet, and I knew that eventually the driver had driven off with Nigella to get the horse-box.

I know that the other horses were frightened and bewildered, and that other people arrived and an elderly woman fainted from shock and had to be laid out on the verge, so that by the time Nigella drove up in the horse-box, it was just like a battle scene with the blood and the smell of sweat and the body on the grass, and the weeping and the wailing, and the anxoius shouts of complete strangers who, never having been close to a horse in their lives before, struggled manfully as people will in times of crisis, to hold on to the hirelings.

There was no time for tears or recriminations as we organized the transportation of the horses back to the stables, first Legend with his sides and his legs caked with blood, then the others by degrees, and ourselves and the shooting brake. It seemed to take forever to achieve all this, but at last it was done and I was standing in the stable holding the sweating, distressed bay gelding, whilst the vet swabbed and stitched and the Fanes stood with pails of bloody water, and Doreen wept silently in a corner until Lady Jennifer came silently into the stable and took her away, gathering her up like an armful of crumpled laundry.

'You're lucky,' the vet said finally, as he stood back to survey his handiwork. 'There's nothing broken and it looked a lot worse than it really was. He's lost a fair amount of blood, but it was a clean injury and not too deep; it shoudn't leave much of a scar. He'll be as good as new in a few months.'

We tried very hard to feel lucky. Afterwards we told ourselves over and over again how lucky we were to have a horse at all, when he could so easily have been irreparably injured or killed, and that the driver of the car could have been injured himself and have decided to sue. It had been luck of a kind, we supposed.

But standing in the lantern-lit stable on the blood-soaked straw, with our hair matted and our cheeks splashed with red, with the vet called from his fireside, and Henrietta in her sticky, striped apron, we didn't feel lucky.

We looked at our bruised and battered horse, and we knew that this was the end of the two-day event, the end of the training scholarship, and for all we knew, the end of an eventing career.

12

A Substitute Eventer

'Elaine,' Nigella said, 'Forster's here.'

Friday night. I had forgotten.

'Tell him to go away,' I said.

'I have,' she said, 'he won't.'

'That's right,' Forster agreed, 'I won't.'

He came into Lady Jennifer's little sitting-room behind Nigella, took her by the waist and placed her outside the door, closing it in her face.

'That wasn't very polite,' I said.

'I'm not a very polite person. What are you doing?'

'I'm writing a letter.' This wasn't exactly true. I was sitting at the bureau with a blank piece of notepaper in front of me and a pen in my hand, but I hadn't started to write, not yet.

Henrietta came in. She was wearing scuffed, pink, stiletto-heeled shoes, lurex tights, her black leg-warmers and a mini-skirt.

'Goodbye, Miss Fane,' Forster said pointedly.

'Oh,' Henrietta said, surprised, 'do you want me to go? I thought I was invited. Before this happened, we were all going out together.'

'All?' Forster looked at me suspiciously. '*All*?'

'Yes,' I said wearily. 'All. It was to be a sort of revenge.'

'I see,' Forster sat down on a small Edwardian chair and rocked back on it, staring at me with narrowed eyes.

'Don't do that,' Henrietta told him, 'you'll break its legs.'

'And if you don't leave the room,' Forster said, in a conversational tone, 'I'll probably break yours.'

'I'd better leave,' Henrietta said apologetically, 'in case he does.' She went out, resigned to more jam making for the Red Cross.

Forster got up and wandered over to the mantelpiece. He

picked up a sepia photograph in a cracked rosewood frame. 'Is this old Lord Fane?'

'It was,' I said. 'He died about ten years ago. He wasn't very good with money; I believe he drank.'

Forster set the photograph down again. 'I should think his family drove him to it.'

'I do wish,' I said, 'that you wouldn't be quite so scathing about the Fanes.'

Forster came over to the bureau. He wasn't dressed for going out. He was wearing cords and a jersey and a Husky waistcoat. 'Who are you writing to?'

'I'm writing to the BHS to resign from the training scholarship,' I said. 'I thought if I wrote straight away, they would have time to invite someone else to the two-day event in my place. I haven't actually started it yet,' I admitted, 'it isn't going to be a very pleasant letter to write.'

'Then don't write it,' he said, 'it isn't a good idea.'

I stared at him curiously. 'What do you mean it isn't a good idea? What did you come for, anyway? You must have heard about the accident. You must have known.'

'Of course I knew,' he said, 'the whole village knew. The whole country probably knows by now.'

'And you knew how I'd be feeling; you knew I wouldn't want to go out?'

'I knew that as well.'

'Yet, you still came?' I said wonderingly.

'I still came.' Forster leaned one elbow on the top of the bureau and rested his chin on his hand. I looked up at him, and he looked levelly back at me.

'You could have gone out with Janie Richardson instead,' I said.

'I could.'

'But you didn't.'

'No, I didn't.'

Henrietta poked her head round the door. 'Would you care for some coffee?' she enquired.

'Go away,' Forster said. He didn't shift his gaze from mine.

The head withdrew. 'If she keeps popping in,' Forster said, 'I might easily break her neck as well as her legs.'

'Why *did* you come?' I said.

'I came,' he said, 'just in time to stop you writing a letter you might regret.' He pulled away the notepaper and crumpled it into a ball in his fist.

'But if I don't write it now,' I said, 'it will still need to be written; if not today, then tomorrow, or the next day, or the next.'

'No,' he said fiercely, 'it needn't!' He hurled the crumpled piece of paper into the fireplace. 'You can't give up as easily as that!'

I looked at him in astonishment, not knowing whether to feel hurt or angry. 'I'm not giving up *easily*,' I told him, 'or because I *want* to, only because I *have* to!'

Forster turned away. He pushed his hands into the pockets of his waistcoat and glowered at the threadbare carpet. 'Elaine,' he said eventually, 'this scholarship means a hell of a lot to you, doesn't it?'

'You mean it did,' I said carefully. 'It would have meant that Legend and I had a really good start, with all the professional help we needed. It would have given us a foot in the door of the eventing world; and of course, it would have been nice to have earned it ourselves, not to have been dependent on the Fanes to finance it. Yes,' I admitted sadly, 'the scholarship meant an awful lot, and I'm very, very sorry to have lost it.'

'But you might not have completely lost it,' he said.

'I could try again next year,' I admitted, 'but the way things are going I might not have a horse next year; if the Fanes get really hard-pressed, Legend could be the first to go.'

'I don't mean next year,' he replied, 'I mean this year. I mean now.'

I looked at him, surprised to find that he still didn't completely understand. 'But I *have*,' I said, 'I've completely lost Legend for this year, he won't be fit enough to do

93

anything at all for at least three months. The two-day event's next week!'

'You've lost Legend, yes, but you could go on another horse, you could take a substitute! They allowed somebody to take a substitute last year; horses are always going lame at the last minute, they accept that!'

'Another horse?' The idea had not crossed my mind. It hadn't occurred to me that I could compete in the two-day event on any horse other than Legend. 'But another horse . . .' I didn't really want to ride another horse; I wouldn't be able to do justice to a strange animal in the short time there was left to train before the competition, and anyway, I couldn't think of a suitable animal to be had.

'I honestly don't think so,' I said, 'if I can't go on Legend . . . there isn't a horse I can think of who could take his place; horses like Legend don't exactly grow on trees, you know, they're very hard to find.'

'I realize that.' Forster stared at the carpet. 'It just seems such a wicked waste of an opportunity,' he said, 'to get so far, and then have to give in.'

'I know,' I said.

'So if there was something, *anything*, that was nearly good enough,' he said, 'at least you wouldn't be out of the running altogether. You'd still have a chance.'

'Yes,' I said doubtfully, 'I suppose I would.'

'After all,' he went on, 'they *are* assessing potential, they must have seen potential in your own performance, and they would certainly have seen it in Legend.'

'I suppose so,' I said.

'And in three months he'll be working again, so the chances are that he'll be completely fit by the time the course begins.' I nodded in agreement. 'So you owe it to everyone to try, to yourself, to Legend, even to the Fanes.'

I frowned. 'Well, if you put it like that . . .'

'Elaine,' Forster said, 'is there no other horse even *remotely* suitable, that you could take to the two-day event?'

I stared at him silently, thinking of a grey horse who never lost his courage, a horse who could gallop, a horse who never, ever, flattened over his fences. It was a risk, I knew, but: 'I do believe,' I said, 'that there is.'

I went into the kitchen. The heat and steam and the sickly smell were overpowering. Lady Jennifer was ladling the Red Cross jam into jars. Henrietta was sitting at the table writing labels with her tongue between her teeth and her hair clinging damply to her forehead in little tendrils. Nigella was weighing sugar.

'Where's Forster?' they wanted to know.

'He's gone,' I said. 'I've just shown him out. And I would like you to know that I'm still going to the two-day event.'

'As a spectator?' Nigella said. 'Won't that be rather depressing?'

'Not as a spectator,' I said, 'as a competitor.'

Henrietta looked up from the labels with her mouth open. 'But you haven't got a horse,' she objected. 'How can you possibly . . .'

'I'm going on The Comet,' I said.

'Not The Comet!' Nigella cried. 'You're not thinking of taking The Comet to the two-day event!'

Henrietta pushed the damp hair off her face and looked at me speculatively. 'What about the cross-country?' she wondered. 'Will he run away?'

I shrugged. 'The only question is, will he run in the right direction?'

'But the schooling,' Nigella cried in agitation, 'and the dressage! Will we have time to prepare?'

'We'll make time,' I said.

I dipped my finger into one of the pots of jam and sucked it reflectively.

Everyone was silent, deliberating this new turn of events. Henrietta had stopped writing labels. Nigella's sugar lay forgotten on the scales. Only Lady Jennifer continued to fill up the jam jars.

'I should think The Comet might be *frightfully* good at eventing,' she said.

95

13

An Evening with the Pony Club

'Are you sure you don't want any help with your dressage, Elaine?' Nigella said. She was walking by my stirrup as we left the little grass rick-yard which made an ideal, enclosed arena for our show-jumps. The Comet had jumped everything we had constructed, steadily and with the minimum of fuss. We had decided not to tempt fate by taking him over the cross-country course in the park; we had had enough anxiety and accidents, and the grey horse's performance over fences at speed had never been in doubt.

'No,' I told Nigella. 'Quite honestly, I would rather work by myself. It's a completely different test, so I'll ride a few movements at a time and learn it as I go along.'

Nigella went off to help Henrietta to hose Legend's legs. He had been on three corn feeds a day at the time of the accident, and the enforced idleness had caused his legs to become puffy and heated. He was now on a non-heating diet of bran, sugar beet pulp and sliced roots and we were hosing each leg with cold water for fifteen minutes twice a day.

I rode The Comet out into the park and began to ride the test through. The hirelings ambled over and stood in an aimless little group outside the markers, watching our circles and our halts, our transitions and our serpentines. The Comet was stiff at first, and uncertain, but as time went on he became better and better and it was clear to me that at some time he had been schooled to a very high standard indeed. I rode him back to the stables, pleased with the way he had performed, but at the same time, slightly troubled.

Before he had left on Friday evening, Nick Forster had asked me out again, and this time I had promised faithfully not to bring the Fanes. I hadn't been looking forward to

96

telling them that I was going out without them, but in the event I was saved by Thunder and Lightning Limited who sent four complimentary tickets for a local DiscoNite at which they were making a live appearance. When I refused mine because I was already going out with Nick, the Fanes decided to give the extra tickets to Doreen and Brenda, so everyone was happy.

When it came to getting ready though, I hadn't a clue what to wear. I looked at the clothes in my worm-eaten wardrobe and I didn't seem to have anything suitable at all.

'Where are you going with Forster,' Henrietta wanted to know, 'that you have to make such a fuss?' Henrietta never made a fuss about clothes. She had thrown together an alarming outfit for the DiscoNite consisting of the lurex tights, the black leg-warmers, an elongated purple jersey that barely covered her thighs, and her scuffed pink satin stiletto shoes.

'I don't know,' I admitted, wondering why on earth I hadn't thought to ask. 'It could be a meal, I suppose, or on the other hand, it could be just a drink at a pub.'

'Or it might be the cinema,' Nigella suggested. She was wearing tight black trousers, her red pill-box, her tap-dancing shoes and a black T-shirt with a moth-hole in the shoulder. 'Why don't you wear this?' She pulled out the only classic garment I possessed, a cream linen suit.

The cream suit was more suitable for a wedding than a drink at a pub, but I struggled into it anyway.

Henrietta considered me with her head on one side. She had back-combed her hair until it stood out beyond her shoulders. Two long, thin plaits hung down in front of each ear. The effect was astonishing.

'You look far too colourless,' she decided, 'with your pale hair and your skin and everything. Can't you find something really bright to cheer yourself up?' She began to rummage through my things in the carved coffin-chest at the foot of my bed. Eventually she came up with a lime-green, nylon jersey. 'Here, try this.'

I tried it. It looked terrible.

'I can't wear this,' I said, 'it looks awful.'

'You're right,' Henrietta agreed. 'It does look awful.'

In the meantime Nigella had vanished in the direction of her own bedroom and returned with a crepe blouse in hot pink with a pie-frill collar and a sash. I put it on and looked in the mirror. The colour was very fierce.

'You still look boring,' Henrietta said. She removed the sash from the waist and tied it round my head as if I was a Red Indian. 'Now that looks much better,' she said approvingly.

'Oh,' I said doubtfully, 'I really don't know if . . .'

'Aren't you going to wear any makeup?' Nigella interrupted. The Fanes had painted kohl around their eyes and vivid blusher on their cheeks. Henrietta had small, metallic stars stuck across her forehead. Standing together they looked rather like a cabaret turn. I was relieved to think I hadn't got to go with them to the DiscoNite.

I used some mascara and some lip gloss. Henrietta brushed aside my objections and applied some of her blusher to my cheeks.

I stared at myself in the spotted mirror. My reflection stared back at me. The sash around my head looked freakish. My cheeks appeared to be burning with a fever. The hot pink blouse didn't help. I ran downstairs. It was too late to do anything about it.

Nick drove down the Fanes' pot-holey drive trying not to lose the exhaust pipe of his white, low-slung, sports car. He looked at me curiously. 'Are you all right, Elaine?' he enquired. 'You look a bit hot and bothered.'

'Yes,' I said brightly, 'I'm fine.' I got out a tissue and rubbed off some of the blusher when he wasn't looking.

We drove out beyond Westbury and turned into the forecourt of a rambling, timbered hotel called the Wild Duck Inn. The car park was overflowing and there were even a couple of coaches.

'It's busier than usual,' Nick commented, 'it's generally

pretty quiet.' He opened my door. 'Do you have to wear that thing round your head?' he said with a trace of anxiety in his voice. 'It looks a bit odd.'

I had forgotten the sash. I snatched it off. 'It was Henrietta's idea,' I apologized.

Nick put his arm around me as we walked towards the main entrance of the hotel. 'I'm glad you didn't decide to invite the Fanes along this time,' he said. 'I'm looking forward to a night on our own.'

I waited in the beamed hall whilst Nick took our jackets to the cloakroom lobby. I felt a bit nervous. I wondered if Nick brought all his girlfriends to the Wild Duck Inn. There was a notice board with posters on it by the reception desk. I wandered over to it and read a few of the announcements just for something to do. Pride of place on the notice board went to a bright orange handbill. It said:

! TONIGHT ! TONIGHT !
The Midvale and Westbury Pony Club
DiscoNite
at the Wild Duck Inn, Fressington,
featuring
THUNDER AND LIGHTNING LIMITED
Live!

This was altogether too terrible to believe. I looked round for Nick, appalled. It would ruin our evening if we were to meet up with the Fanes. I had to tell him that we must leave at once. 'Nick,' I said urgently, 'Nick, we . . .' but the district commissioner clapped a welcoming hand on each of our shoulders. 'Jolly noble of you to support our little effort what? what?' he shouted. 'Should make a tidy sum tonight if we all live through it, eh? eh?' He laughed energetically at his own joke and steered us firmly into a nearby bar where the Pony Club committee appeared to be bent upon consuming the maximum amount of beer in the shortest possible time. Nick gave me a despairing look as we were separated by a raucous group of Pony Club associates. Pints flew back and forth. A martini was thrust into my hand and the district commissioner began a shouted conversation about the necessity of giving the members what they wanted, even if it perforated their eardrums in the process; all modern groups, he bellowed, were either damned louts or fairies, and Thunder and Ligh3ning Limited were no bloody different. Whether they hunted or not, a spell in the blasted army would do them a power of good.

I listened to all this and I wondered how we could possibly make our escape. The district commissioner regarded the hunt servants as his own personal property. Not only that, but his brother-in-law was master of the Hunt and I knew that Nick couldn't afford to offend him. After a while, the district commissioner clapped his hands which seemed to be the signal for a general exodus to the DiscoNite. Nick managed to make his way to my side.

'We'll go in with them,' he whispered, 'then we'll leave; it's sure to be dark, they'll never notice.' He squeezed my hand reassuringly.

In the ballroom where the DiscoNite was being held, it was pitch black except for a myriad of coloured lights pulsating to the beat of the terrifyingly loud music produced by the band. Thunder and Ligh3ning Limited had been bald when we had first known them, now they had their hair dragged up to form a central spike dyed in alternate colours of orange, green, red and blue. They pranced and strutted across the stage wearing leather knee-breeches and bolero tops with flashes of lightning appliqued on to them. Their chests and their arms and legs looked hatefully white and puny and it was all simply hideous.

I could tell that Nick loathed it. We stumbled in the wake of the district commissioner who led us to some tables situated as far away from the band as he could get. Someone slapped drinks on to the table in front of us. The district commissioner sat down at the next table. 'Rather like being in hell what? what?' he bellowed. He took some cotton wool out of his pocket and stuffed it into his ears, prepared to sit it out until the bitter end. Conversation was virtually impossible.

Nick and I began to plot our departure in sign language. We would get up and pretend to dance, working our way towards the exit, then we would make a bolt for it. We started to rise, but: 'Well, if it isn't Busy Bee!' a fog horn voice proclaimed, and Brenda, vast in what appeared to be a pair of lilac pyjamas, plonked herself down at our table, making it rock, and spilling our drinks. Nick, who had hitherto kept his temper under trying circumstances, set his lips in a tight line. Brenda's face was plastered with her usual brand of orange panstick and her bleached, white hair was slicked flat on to her scalp like a bathing cap.

'What's going on here, Busy Bee?' she bellowed. 'Sitting in the dark with Lover Boy, are we?'

'Look, Brenda,' Nick said threateningly, 'take yourself off somewhere else. Elaine and I were having a private conversation.'

'Private seduction, more like!' Brenda hooted. 'You want to watch this lady killer, Busy Bee; if half what I've heard about him's true, he'll . . .'

Any further revelations were cut short by the arrival of Henrietta in the elongated purple jersey.

'Oh God,' Forster said, aghast, 'not *you*.'

'Why shouldn't it be me?' Henrietta demanded indignantly, 'I hardly expected to see you here, and Elaine knew *we* were coming.'

Forster stared across the table at me in disbelief. His face in the disco lights went from red to orange to green. I looked at him helplessly, unable to deny it. Nigella appeared wearing the red pill-box with the veil, and with her came Doreen in tartan knickerbockers.

'Come and join the party,' Brenda boomed, 'the drinks are on Lover Boy!'

'Oh, thank you,' Nigella said, gratefully sinking into a chair. 'I'll have a campari and soda.'

Henrietta and Doreen seated themselves expectantly at the table. Nick shot Brenda a venomous look and went to fetch the drinks. No sooner had he regained his seat than

William arrived, very red about the neck, and two steps behind him came Janie Richardson. Far from being delighted, Nick sprang to his feet looking enraged. 'What the bloody hell's going on?' he shouted at William. 'What's *she* doing here?'

It was all very awkward. Janie Richardson sat down opposite me and stared round the table in an unfriendly manner. She was wearing a tight, silver dress and her hair was like a black bush. I thought it had looked a lot better under the silk hat.

Behind my back William was trying to explain himself to Nick. 'She rang up after you'd left,' he hissed. 'I told her you were fixed up, but you know what she's like. She guessed you'd be here, and she asked me to bring her; I didn't want to come, but I couldn't very well refuse, *could* I?'

'I'm sorry about all this,' Janie Richardson said, not looking it, 'but the thing is that Nick was supposed to have been with me tonight.'

'Is that so?' Henrietta exclaimed, pulling up her chair in an interested manner. 'I thought he was rather keen on Elaine, he's been chasing her for ages.'

'Of course, he could quite easily be attracted to two people,' Nigella pointed out in a reasonable tone. 'After all, he doesn't actually have to choose; it isn't like getting engaged or anything.'

'That's not very fair though, that isn't,' Doreen put in, 'asking one girl out then taking another. I'd chuck him, Elaine, if I was you.'

I wondered how much more of this I could stand. Things were getting pretty heated behind me, and William might well have ended up with a thump on his nose but for the district commissioner who suddenly spotted him and rose from his seat, overjoyed at having both whippers-in attending his DiscoNite. He clapped William affectionately on his back.

'Hunt jolly well represented tonight, what? what?' he whooped. 'Got to support the young entry, eh? eh?'

This distraction gave Brenda the opportunity she had been waiting for. 'Now look here, Cassanova,' she said to Nick in a belligerent voice. 'What the devil are you up to, asking Busy Bee out, when you're supposed to be with her?' She pointed to Janie, who jumped up from her seat and threw herself at Nick, unexpectedly bursting into loud sobs. Everyone at the table who had previously been riveted by the turn of events, now looked embarrassed.

'Mind your own bloody business, Brenda,' Nick said furiously, and taking Janie Richardson by the elbow, he steered her away, through the dancers and out of the exit, without even a backward glance.

'Well,' Brenda said in disgust, 'I bet that's the last we'll see of *him* tonight.'

William did his best to apologize. 'I'm very sorry, Elaine,' he said, looking scarlet and very ill-at-ease. 'It was my fault for bringing her, but she made me, she's ever so persistent.'

I could believe it, but now I felt horribly unwanted, abandoned and miserable. How could I, in my plain, cream skirt and the unflattering, hot pink blouse, hope to compete with the exotic Janie Richardson with her coal black locks and her silver dress? I knew I couldn't, and the thought of it made me feel ill. 'I want to go home,' I said.

'You can come home with us,' Nigella said comfortingly. 'Brenda's driving; but we can't go yet, Henrietta's going to sing.'

As she spoke, the deafening music suddenly died away and Solly Chell, the drummer with Thunder and Lighʒning Limited came to the edge of the stage and squinted into the interrupted dancers. 'You there, 'Enry?' he bawled. 'You ready?'

Henrietta jumped up, startled, and scampered off towards the stage. Everyone got up to follow, determined to have a better view. I followed them, not really wanting to, but not wanting to be left like a wall-flower with the district commissioner either.

Johnny Jones, the lead singer, handed the microphone to

Henrietta. If I had been feeling less wretched, I might have been excited and even nervous for her. Henrietta sang all the time around the stables, composing little songs of her own to suit the occasion. We were so used to it that we no longer noticed, but we had never before heard her sing with the band – only informally, in the cab of the horse-box, driving home after hunting.

The band crashed into an introduction. The lights pulsed. The accompaniment was ear-piercing and strident, but Henrietta's clear voice soared above it. Even the youngest members of the pony club stopped yelling and listened. Everybody was entranced by the girl who stood in front of the band and sang like a lark. In her eccentric clothes, and totally unafraid, she could have been a pop star, yet somehow she managed to be nothing like one.

Intent on Henrietta's performance in spite of myself, I felt an arm steal round my waist. 'I'm sorry it took so long,' Nick whispered into my ear, 'but I had to tell her once and for all that it was no good. She was a bit upset. I had to get her a taxi.'

I felt weak with relief. I should have known he would come back. Now that he was standing beside me, I wondered how I could possibly have doubted it. We smiled into each other's eyes and joined in the appreciative hullaballoo for the girl in the elongated purple jersey as she jumped down from the stage.

14

Welcome to the Two-Day Event

'Welcome, welcome, everyone!' The portly figure of Felix Hissey stood on a small, raised platform which had been erected between the scoreboards. The familiar, ruddy-cheeked face which beamed from millions of pickle jars and sauce bottles on kitchen tables and supermarket shelves, now beamed down at us in person. 'Welcome, welcome!' cried Felix Hissey again.

'Oh, do get on with it,' Henrietta muttered impatiently. She had only half-plaited The Comet's mane, and was dying to get back to finish it.

'Welcome,' Felix Hissey said, clasping his chubby hands together in delight, 'to this very special two-day event, and a most special welcome to the Hissey Training Scholarship Candidates!'

We were back on the combined training competition ground, this time for the two-day event. In the box, The Comet waited; his fading dapples had been shampooed, his tail dipped in blue-bag, his hooves had been scrubbed, even the whiskers had been trimmed from his nose. He had submitted himself to all these attentions with his customary disregard and now, with his mane half-plaited, he waited for whatever might come next.

'And welcome,' the King of Pickle continued throwing out his arms towards us in a gesture of universal joy and friendship, 'to all the other competitors today, who have so sportingly agreed to make up the numbers; welcome! Welcome to you all!' He beamed round expansively once more, and clambered down from the platform to a scattering of applause.

'Is that it?' Nigella wondered. 'Can we go ?' But the chief of the selection committee was now on the platform.

The chief wore cavalry twill trousers with knife-edge creases, a Tattersalls check shirt and a BHS tie. He stared at us crossly, as if we had no right to be there at all, which was something of a shock, coming after Felix Hissey.

'The dressage will begin in exactly half an hour,' he rapped, throwing up his chin in a defensive manner as if to stall any attempt at argument. 'We expect every person to be riding in within sight of the starting steward at least fifteen minutes prior to their allotted time!'

'He makes it sound like a court-martial,' Henrietta muttered.

'There will be an interval for lunch at one o'clock and the show-jumping will begin at two o'clock sharp!' The chief narrowed his eyes at us, as if we might regard this as unreasonable and begin to throw things. 'Competitors will jump in reverse result order!' he barked.

'He might not be as bad as he seems,' Nigella whispered. 'He's probably very fond of dogs and small children, most of these BHS types are.'

I couldn't imagine it.

'Accommodation for the horses belonging to the scholarship candidates has been arranged at the manor stables,' continued the chief. 'There is also dormitory accommodation for the candidates themselves if required!' He threw up his chin again and glared around as if challenging anyone to dare to apply for it. 'There will be a veterinary inspection at nine o'clock tomorrow morning, the cross-country phase will begin at ten o'clock prompt, and there will be a short presentation ceremony at four-thirty!' Having delivered the last of the information at lightning speed, he walked sideways off the platform as if he suspected that there might be snipers in the audience.

'Are you nervous?' Nigella asked, as we made our way back to the horse-box. 'You don't appear to be.' She looked at me curiously, 'you don't appear to be worried at all.'

In some strange way I wasn't. It was as if all the happenings of the past few weeks had exhausted my capacity

106

for worrying. The part of me that should have been worrying about the dressage, the show-jumping, the cross-country course, and the possible consequences of what I was doing, had run dry. There wasn't any worry left. 'I'm not worried,' I said, 'not any more.'

As it was half term, Doreen was with us and she led The Comet down the ramp of the horse-box. Henrietta opened her plaiting box and began to sew up the rest of his mane. We had plenty of time, The Comet didn't need very much preparatory schooling. I put on my navy jacket and my hat, Doreen pulled off the tail bandage and brushed out The Comet's tail. Nigella tacked up.

'It's remarkable that the saddle we bought for Legend fits so well,' she commented, as she ducked under The Comet's belly to catch the girth. 'It might have been made for him.'

The Comet stood like a rock at the top end of the dressage arena; he stared into the distance, beyond the judges and their writers in the Range Rover, beyond the Jacobean manor house with its twisted chimneys and its topiary, even beyond the horizon. It seemed to me, waiting at A, that he might possibly never move again, but he was ready the second I closed my legs against his sides to begin the test.

Riding the test seemed to be more of a dream than reality. It slipped along quickly and effortlessly. I was conscious only of the flexing of the powerful neck contained by the unfamiliar double bridle, the grey ears set firmly forward, the scrubbed hooves flying in extension, thudding gently in canter, plated four-square on the turf at the halt. It all seemed so incredibly easy on the wise, grey horse, but then, I told myself, as we left the arena at a swinging walk on a long rein, he had probably done it all so very many times before.

For some reason known only to the chief, the dressage scores were not posted until all the tests had been ridden. Even before the last horse had left the arena, little knots of

107

anxious people had gathered silently around the scoreboards.

The chief finally emerged from the secretary's tent with the result sheet in one hand and a stick of chalk in the other. He gave us a few sharp looks, climbed on to a chair, whipped round in order to ascertain that none of us had found this amusing, threw up his chin, and began to write.

The scholarship candidates' numbers were underlined in red to distinguish them from the non-participating competitors. The first candidate's score was 111, the next 94, then 101, then 89. 'That's the best scholarship score so far,' Nigella commented in a nervous voice; then as a 77 was posted, 'that's better still.'

Henrietta was quite unable to speak. She gazed intently at the board and picked furiously at the sleeve of her jersey. As we watched, the chief posted a score of 92 against another candidate's number; then he posted mine, 57.

The chief wrote it, looked at it, consulted the result sheet to check that he hadn't made a mistake, then threw up his chin and carried on scoring. When he had entered all the marks, he dismounted from the chair, looked quickly round for signs of rebellion, and observing none, vanished smartly into the secretary's tent.

The Fanes simply couldn't believe it. They stared at the scoreboard with their mouths open.

'Fifty-seven,' Henrietta said incredulously, '*fifty-seven?*'

'It isn't possible,' Nigella said in bewilderment. 'They couldn't have given The Comet fifty-seven; there must have been a mix-up on the score sheets, someone must have made a mistake.'

I knew there had been no mistake; fifty-seven was a fair mark for the kind of test The Comet had performed. He was older, he was not as supple, not as schooled, not as brilliant as he once had been, but it had been an admirable test, worthy of fifty-seven. 'He deserved it,' I told them, 'it was a good test.'

'It's not just a *good* test, it's incredible!' cried Henrietta.

'You've got the most fantastic lead! The nearest mark is seventy-seven; you're twenty points ahead! The others will *never* catch you up!'

'I don't suppose they will,' I said, but then, remembering the set of the iron neck, the plank-like jaw, and the awful relentlessness of the grey horse's gallop, I added: 'Unless we break our necks on the cross-country course.'

We made our way towards the trestle tables set out around one of the ancient oak trees, where Felix Hissey was welcoming everyone to participate in his free luncheon. Doreen had almost finished hers. There was a powerful smell of pickled onions.

15

If You're in a Pickle

'Whatever you do,' Henrietta said anxiously, 'don't give him the *slightest* chance to get away from you, keep him *really* collected. Once he gets his neck out, you'll have no chance of stopping him at all.'

'I wonder if I should tighten the curb-chain another link?' Nigella fretted at The Comet's immobile head, slipping her fingers behind the curb-chain to satisfy herself that it was tight enough, and pulling up the cheeks of the curb to test its efficiency. The Comet tried not to notice, concentrating his attention on the far distance, where tiny specks of traffic were visible, moving across the horizon.

'I think you should both stop fussing,' I said. 'He isn't going to run away.'

Because of the reverse result order, I was last to go in the show-jumping. There had been ten clear rounds so far, six of them by short-listed candidates. The liver chestnut gelding inside the ropes took off too close to a white-painted gate and brought it thudding down. He had looked set for another clear, and a sympathetic groan went up from the small crowd of spectators seated on canvas chairs under an awning fronted by a banner which proclaimed *If You're in a Pickle - Make sure it's Hissey's!*

I could see the rotund figure of Felix Hissey himself seated under the awning. He was talking to Nick. As I gazed at them in an abstracted manner, my attention was suddenly caught by two people seated by them; two people whose faces were alarmingly familiar.

'Nigella,' I said in dismay, 'isn't that . . .?' But the liver chestnut gelding was cantering out of the ring and now there was no time. The ring steward called out my number. The Comet and I trotted into the ring. I pushed him into a canter and we circled around, waiting for the bell. The Comet was perfectly calm, perfectly manageable. As I had known he would, he cantered purposefully through the start, taking all the jumps in his stride, soaring over them accurately and obediently to finish with a clear round, well within the time allowed.

As we cantered through the finish I glanced into the crowd under the awning. Nick looked pleased, Felix Hissey was clapping his hands in delight. The two seats which had been occupied by the familiar-looking people were now empty. I closed my eyes and whispered a little prayer for myself and The Comet; praying that I had imagined it; that Lala Thornapple and the nurse had never been there at all.

The Fanes and I hadn't liked the sound of the dormitory accommodation; we had brought sleeping-bags and we were going to spend the night in the horse-box. Felix Hissey was providing a fork supper for everyone under the awning and Henrietta, Nigella and Doreen had gone off to investigate this, leaving me to take The Comet over to his stable at the manor.

On the way I stopped in the shadow of a small spinney to allow The Comet to graze. But The Comet preferred to stand and stare into the spinney, so we both stood and stared into the spinney, made ghostly by its silver birch trees, and I leaned on the fence, listening to the small sounds of life around us, and The Comet's breathing.

'Elaine?'

Someone called my name softly. It was Nick, creeping up behind us like a thief in the night. He came and rested his arms on the fence beside me. We stood for quite a while, looking into the spinney with The Comet standing silently beside us. 'Have you walked the course for tomorrow?' Nick wanted to know.

I told him that the Fanes and I had walked it earlier, all four miles and twenty-eight fences of it, through woodland, over grass and along tracks. I wanted to say more, I wished with all my heart that I could confide in Nick, that I could tell him what I had begun to suspect and ask him what I should do, but all of this was made impossible by his friendship with Felix Hissey. So everything I might have said remained unspoken, and I stared into the spinney, thinking, but unable to speak.

'If you're worried about the cross-country,' he said, 'I'll be there. I'll be driving Felix round in the Range Rover; if anything happens, if the old horse takes off, I won't be far behind.'

'Thanks,' I said, 'I appreciate it.' My voice sounded distant, even to my own ears.

'Elaine,' Nick said gently, 'what's the matter?'

'Why should anything be the matter?' I said. I blinked furiously, glad of the shadows, quite unable to cope with sympathy.

'You've won the dressage by a huge margin, you got a clear round in the show-jumping,' he said, 'aren't you even pleased?'

'Of course I'm pleased,' I answered . 'Why wouldn't I be?'

'Because something tells me that you're not,' he said, 'something tells me that you're not pleased at all.' He removed his elbows from the fence and turned his back on me, staring across the shadowy park towards the distant crowd of people gathered around the awning. 'Something tells me that you're sorry you came, sorry I even suggested it'.

There was nothing I could say to this. I just stared down at the long, lush grass growing beside the spinney, grass that The Comet didn't want. 'I don't want you to think I'm not grateful,' I said, 'because I am.'

'I don't want you to be grateful,' Nick said, his voice low and angry. 'I just want to know what's gone wrong between us in the space of a few days. I thought we understood each other after the other night; I thought there was something definite between us. Now I'm not so sure.'

'It isn't anything to do with you and me,' I told him. 'It's nothing to do with the way I feel. After all this is over, I might be able to tell you and then you'll understand.'

'And perhaps I won't,' he said wearily. 'I can't understand you, Elaine. I'm not even sure that I want to try.'

I didn't call after him as he walked away. After a while I continued on my way towards the stables behind the Jacobean house with its twisted chimneys black against the sky. The Comet walked beside me; he wasn't exactly invisible, but he was as insubstantial as a ghost or a memory in the twilight.

'If all this fails,' Henrietta said, as she knelt at The Comet's feet and sewed up his bandages, 'and something terrible happens today, we can always go back to fund-raising, and show-jump The Comet. I can't imagine why we haven't thought of it before.'

'We haven't thought of it before,' Nigella pointed out in a harassed voice, 'because he's a bolter.' She was very het-up about the cross-country. She pulled up the surcingle and slipped The Comet's rubber-covered reins under the stirrups and leathers. 'Are you *positively* sure you don't want the double bridle, Elaine?' she asked me for the umpteenth time. 'I'm sure you won't be able to hold him in the snaffle.'

'The snaffle's fine,' I assured her. 'I can't possibly risk taking him in a double, I woudn't be able to cope with all those reins, especially when they get slippery with sweat, and anyway, I wouldn't want to risk hurting his mouth. I'm sure to get left behind over a couple of fences.'

'Hurt The Comet's mouth?' Henrietta exclaimed incredulously. 'What a joke!'

I pulled on my navy guernsey and slipped my number-cloth over it. Doreen stood by holding my safety helmet and the cross-country starting times. The horses were being sent off at five minute intervals and I was the last one to go. I had less than half an hour to prepare.

Nigella was working herself up into a state of total panic. 'Do we need over-reach boots?' She began to fling various articles of tack out of the locker in a frantic effort to locate them.

'If she's looking for over-reach boots,' Henrietta called, 'tell her they're here, on the ramp.'

'What about vaseline?' Nigella wanted to know. 'Do we need to vaseline his legs?' She ran to the back of the horse-box in order to consult *Training the Event Horse*. It had lost its dust jacket and there was hoof oil on the cover. I couldn't imagine what the library were going to say when, or if, she ever returned it.

'Please don't panic,' I said. 'There's no need. It's going to be all right, honestly.' I could remember Nigella saying similar reassuring things to me at the Point-to-Point. It seemed ironic that I should be repeating them now. 'I'm not going to get bolted with, we're not going to fall, nothing is going to happen to us.'

Nigella stared at me. Two bright spots of colour burned on her cheeks. 'How can you possibly know what is or isn't going to happen?' she demanded. 'Why are you suddenly so confident?'

I put on my safety helmet and fastened the chin strip. I couldn't tell her why. 'It isn't a difficult course,' I said, 'it isn't exactly Badminton.' I strapped my watch to my wrist and wrote my starting and finishing times on my shirt cuff with a ballpoint pen.

As I went to mount, I saw that Nigella had left *Training the Event Horse* open on the ramp. Genesis was there for all to see, being hung with laurel wreathes after his victory in the Olympics. I tipped the book closed with my boot. It toppled off the side of the ramp and landed in the water bucket. Nigella fished it out, appalled.

'They'll make you pay for it now,' Doreen informed her. 'They won't take it back, they're ever so fussy, libraries are.'

I took The Comet's rubber-covered reins from under the leathers and pulled down the irons. 'I wouldn't worry,' I said. 'I doubt if we'll need it after today.'

Horses trickled home as The Comet and I waited for the signal to start. Horses returned dripping with sweat, with pumping sides and gusting breath, horses returned lame,

114

others flew through the finish with their heads in the air, looking as if they would do it all again. Their riders looked red-faced, hot and triumphant, or pale and strained; one returned sodden from a ducking, slipping and squelching like wash-leather in the saddle, another came on foot and in tears, leading a horse with a twisted front shoe, comforted by parents.

The Fanes stood to one side looking fraught and anxious and five minutes seemed like fifty, but at last the flag was dropped, the stopwatch started, and The Comet and I were cantering away down the hill towards the first fence.

Over the first and the second fences The Comet flew, his bandaged legs settling into a regular, strong gallop, his steady head, pricked ears and his firm, plaited neck reassuringly familiar. Down towards the first drop fence he went, steadying with his powerful shoulders, jumping down and down and putting in a stride between the fences and down and down again, then up a short incline and over the tallest but least awkward of the Helsinki steps, just as I had planned it; then a stiff gallop and a huge leap over a hog's back constructed from telegraph poles, and on again, settling into the steady rhythmic gallop, following the orange direction flags down to the water.

It was here that The Comet and I met our first problem. The bed of the swift-running river was sandy, and as The Comet landed he pecked badly as his front feet sank and stuck in the sand.

I flew out of the saddle and up his neck, only saved from a soaking as he threw up his head in a valiant effort to pull out his front feet, and knocked me backwards into the saddle again, plunging forward and cantering gamely across the shallows. I had lost my reins and one stirrup, I was splashed and almost blinded by the water, but pushed onwards by my flailing legs, The Comet leapt up the sleeper-faced bank on to dry land. I barely had time to recover my lost iron and my reins before we were over a stone wall, racing over four timber fences set for galloping, and into the woodland.

115

In the woodland it was dry and dense. The track was twisting and narrow and it was impossible to gallop. It was very silent and I was conscious of The Comet's laboured breathing, of my own breathless gasps, and the crackle and crunch of dead twigs and leaves under the steadily cantering hooves. It was quite a surprise to be suddenly confronted with a post and railed ditch with a jump judge sitting solemnly beside it on a shooting stick. The Comet put on a spurt and lengthened into it, managing to retain enough impulsion to carry us over the wide, low hedge which followed on immediately afterwards, bringing us into a lane with an unexpected clatter of hooves.

Made cautious by recent experience, we approached the second river crossing with care, trotting up to it slowly and dropping off the bank, fully expecting the bed to be soft; it was hard. We splashed across to the opposite bank making watery clopping sounds on the river bed, and jumped out over a low rail. After a gate, a wicket fence, a small bank, and a tight double constructed out of two fallen trees, we were approaching the zig-zag rails and only eight fences from home.

The zig-zag rails had been the fence I had not liked the look of when we had walked the course the previous day. They were a Z shape of silver birch poles and we had to jump all three poles. Cantering up to it, it looked an impossible mass of angles and I tried desperately to remember exactly where I had planned to jump each one. I needn't have worried; The Comet made nothing of it. Jumping exactly where I asked him, slipping in an extra stride here, and lengthening a stride there, he sailed over like the veteran he was, never faltering, as we went on to clear the elephant trap with its sloping gate and yawning pit, up and launching into space over the ski-jump, then down, down, a seemingly endless succession of drop fences with the Fanes and Doreen standing at the bottom. I was feeling tired now, and even The Comet's powerful stride was beginning to flag, but as we breasted the hill and the bandaged legs flew stoutly onwards towards the quarry steps I saw the Range Rover cruising along about a hundred yards away, and looking up the hill, I could see little knots of people under the oak trees. We were approaching the run in.

We pinged through the bullfinch and cleared the chicken coops, there was nothing in front of us now but a level sweep of turf and the finishing posts. There was no danger, though, of The Comet starting to accelerate; he had no reserve left. He couldn't have bolted to save his life. We cantered in wearily to the finish, level with the Range Rover, out of which the Fanes and Doreen and Felix Hissey and Nick tumbled, flinging themselves at The Comet, slapping his wet, hot, sticky neck, shouting their congratulations.

Everyone crowded round, wanting to touch the exhausted grey horse with his sides heaving like a bellows, as if he was a good luck charm. Even the chief was there, barking 'Well done!' and 'Jolly good effort!' Felix Hissey clasped his hands and cried 'Wonderful! Wonderful!' The Fanes were jumping up and down with excitement and Doreen was trying to get through the crowd with rugs for The Comet, sniffing and wiping away tears with the back of her hands, overcome by the emotion of the moment.

It would have been marvellous but for the small, determined figure who came running and pushing through the throng, hotly pursued by another figure in a dark blue dress with black shoes and stockings. Lala Thornapple hurled herself at The Comet's lowered and dripping head, clutching wildly at him with her crippled, twisted hands. 'Genesis!' she cried, 'I knew it was you the minute I saw you! I knew it!'

The chief looked at the grey horse, and at me, and at Lala Thornapple, and his chin flew up and down, and the nurse stared at me, appalled. 'Tell her it isn't true,' she pleaded, 'tell her it's impossible.'

I slipped down from the saddle, ran up the stirrups, unbuckled the surcingle and the girth. I lifted off the saddle and placed it into Nigella's frozen, stupefied arms. I took the rug from Doreen, standing like a village idiot, with her mouth agape, and threw it over The Comet.

'I think she might be right,' I told them, 'I think The Comet is Genesis.'

16
What Do We Do Now?

I stood in front of the selection committee in the secretary's tent and they all stared at me, their faces registering disbelief, irritation, and disappointment. Outside, a small crowd of competitors and their supporters waited, impatient, watchful and muttering.

'And you actually admit,' a tall, thin woman with greying hair said in a perplexed voice, 'that you substituted the grey horse for your own, knowing perfectly well that he was an ex-Olympic eventer ?'

'My own horse was injured, ' I said, 'he was knocked down by a car. He won't be fit to start work again for three months, and The Comet was the only other horse available. If I hadn't decided to come on him, I would have had to resign from the scholarship, but I didn't want to do that; I really needed to win a place,' I added despondently. 'I really wanted to. We all did.' I thought of Legend with his leg inflated like a balloon, of the Fanes waiting dejectedly outside, and even of Nick, who had done his best, but who would quite possibly never want to speak to me again.

'But you did *know*,' another BHS type said, his eyes incredulous, 'that the horse you entered as The Comet was, in fact, not The Comet at all, but Genesis?'

'I didn't know for sure,' I said, 'I only suspected. I'd seen the photographs in the book, and in Lala Thornapple's house, but I didn't know *absolutely*, not for certain, not until after the dressage. I'd guessed by then; I'm not very experienced you see, I haven't been properly trained in advanced riding, and I knew he couldn't have performed a test like that unless he was a very brilliant, exceptional horse.'

'And the owners?' the tall, thin woman said. 'Did the previous owners know? Did they tell you?'

'The previous owners hadn't a clue,' I said. 'To them he was just an old grey horse who jumped like a stag, but had a reputation for being a bolter; he didn't look like an Olympic champion, there was nothing about him to suggest it. He was always very reserved, a secretive sort of horse . . .'

'And you didn't think to mention it to them?'

'No,' I said. 'I wasn't sure anyway, until yesterday, and they would only have laughed. They wouldn't have believed it, nobody would.'

Felix Hissey leaned across the trestle table. For once he wasn't beaming and his round eyes were worried. 'What about young Forster, Miss Would-Be-Event-Rider?' he asked. 'Did you tell him?'

I had expected this. I couldn't bear the thought of Nick being implicated in any way. 'You must believe me when I tell you that I didn't say a word to him about it,' I said. 'Nick Forster knew nothing.'

Felix Hissey leaned back in his chair, satisfied. 'I believe you,' he said. 'I know you, Miss Would-Be-Event-Rider, and I know you wouldn't lie.'

I looked at him gratefully. Nothing about Felix Hissey was a pretence. He was a genuinely nice man.

'You do know,' the chief barked, throwing up his chin and glaring at me as if there was a chance I might deny it, 'that the scholarship was intended for *potential* event horses and riders, *potential,* not proven?'

'I did know,' I agreed, 'it was in the conditions of entry.'

'So you knew you were breaking the rules?'

'It wasn't quite as straightforward as that,' I objected. 'I suspected that I might be, but I couldn't be sure, and all the time I hoped that I was mistaken.'

'But you weren't mistaken, Miss Would-Be-Event-Rider, were you?' Felix Hissey said, scratching his round head in an abstracted manner. 'You weren't mistaken at all.'

'The question is,' the tall, thin woman said, 'what do we do now?'

The selection committee looked baffled.

120

'She'll have to be eliminated from the competition,' the BHS man said eventually, 'and she'll have to be disqualified from the training scholarship. It's really most unfortunate for all concerned, but there's no way round it that I can see.'

I was hardly surprised. It was no more than I expected, and probably less than I deserved.

'I think you had better go outside,' the tall, thin woman said, not unkindly, 'whilst we talk it over.'

I turned to leave, hating the thought of emerging from the tent in front of all those curious and accusing eyes. But the chief sprang to his feet, ready to direct a strategic manoeuvre. He unlaced a flap in the rear of the tent, stuck out his head to ascertain that the coast was clear, then propelled me through it. 'Make a run for it, girl!' he rapped. 'Can't have you running the gauntlet; we'll detail someone to tell your friends.'

I bolted for the horse-box, reflecting that the BHS knew what they were doing when they appointed men like the chief.

'I just don't know what to say to you, Elaine,' Lala Thornapple said, and her eyes, despite the pink-flushed cheeks, were contrite. 'I've been in to see the selection committee and I've told them that you couldn't have known for sure that the horse was Genesis. How could you? You had never seen him in your life before, except in a photograph!' She ran her crooked hands through the grey horse's mane, still crimped from its plaits. 'Why, who would have thought that he would have still been going strong after all this time? But then,' she added fondly, 'he always was the most amazing horse.'

'Why did you part with him?' Nigella wanted to know. 'How could you have sold him, loving him as much as you did?'

'I didn't, ' Lala Thornapple said. 'I went into hospital for an operation on my hands. It was unsuccessful, and the surgeon told my husband that I would never regain the use

121

of them. He didn't want me to ride again after that, knowing that I would never be fully in control, especially on a horse like Genesis. He sold them all before I came home; I expect he thought he was acting for the best.'

We fell silent, imagining Lala Thornapple coming home to an empty stable yard; finding all her beloved horses gone. No wonder she hadn't been able to accept it; no wonder she had been forced to pretend.

'I tried to trace them afterwards,' she said, 'but it was hopeless. Most of them went abroad, as they often do, top class horses like mine; the English can't afford them. The money was well invested; it keeps me in comfort now, I suppose. My husband died soon afterwards.'

'And The Comet just got sold on,' I said, 'getting more and more of a reputation as he went.'

'He always was a very strong horse,' Lala Thornapple said, 'but I can imagine that if anyone took him hunting or anything like that, there would be no holding him; and once it got to be a habit, well, you know what horses are . . .'

'And we bought him,' Henrietta said in wonder. 'But we never guessed; we never knew.'

'And Elaine got him in lieu of wages,' Nigella said. 'It's almost unbelievably ironical that she should end up with an ex-international eventer, without even realizing it.'

'And for him to end up wearing his own saddle,' I said, 'that's the most unbelievable thing of all!'

'I want to ask you, Elaine, my dear,' Lala Thornapple said, 'if you would consider selling Genesis back to me. It would make me so happy; he could have his old stable back, and no horse in the world would be better cared for.'

i knew this was true. I had known that Lala Thornapple was going to ask, so I was prepared for it. The nurse and I had discussed it previously and she had assured me that it would be the best thing possible for Lala Thornapple to have the real Genesis in the stables. I had thought carefully about The Comet and his future. I knew we couldn't use him as a hireling any more, he had caused too many accidents in the past and anyway, he deserved better than that. Today had also shown me that he was too old now for hard work, his heart and his gallant spirit were willing, but his legs were hot and puffy under his support bandages. Yet now the time had come to part with him, I loved him too much to let him go, and the fact that I knew he would walk away without a backward glance only made it harder to bear.

'I'll lend him to you,' I said, 'I don't want to sell him to you because . . .' I tailed off, not liking to finish, not wanting to say because you won't live for ever, and what will become of the old grey horse then, left alone in the empty stable yard.

'I know what you're thinking,' Lala Thornapple said, 'you think I'll die and he'll be sold again. Well,' she sighed, and made a small gesture of resignation with her gnarled hands, 'I'll die, I suppose, but if you agree to part with him, I'll make a will leaving him to you, together with enough money to keep him in comfort until the end of his days.' She looked at me, and her eyes were round and anxious. 'How would that be?'

I looked at the nurse in gratitude, knowing that this had been her doing. 'I think that would be very satisfactory,' I said.

'Welcome, Welcome!' cried Felix Hissey. 'Welcome to this final prize-giving ceremony! Welcome to you all!'

We stood at the foot of the raised platform waiting to hear the results. Nobody had either confirmed or denied that I had been disqualified from both the competition and the scholarship, but I knew that I must have been. Knowingly or unknowingly, I had broken the rules, and that seemed all there was to it.

'The results of the two-day event are as follows,' Felix Hissey beamed down at me in what appeared to be an encouraging manner. My heart lifted slightly, then plummeted. 'In first place with seventy-seven penalty points, Mrs Zara Gibbons' Flame Thrower, ridden by Selena Gibbons!'

A delighted cheer went up from the crowd. One or two people nearby turned to stare at me curiously; they knew that something had gone wrong, but they didn't know what.

'In second place,' Felix Hissey announced, 'Harvest Moon, ridden and owned by Timothy Whate!' Another cheer went up. I wondered if I could creep away without attracting too much attention, but decided that I couldn't. The Fanes and Doreen stood stoutly by my side; if they could stand it, then so could I.

'In third place,' Felix Hissey continued, 'Edwin Drood, owned and ridden by Mary Ann Maddox! In fourth place, Mrs Greta Shannon's Brown Paper Parcel, ridden by Davina Shannon! And fifth, Master Facey Romford, owned and ridden by Phillip Hastings! Finally,' he cried, slapping his hands in a joyous manner, 'in sixth place, Fox Me, owned and ridden by Amanda Willis!'

I joined in the general applause, feeling desolate. I hadn't expected to have been allowed to win; my own sense of fair play told me that it wouldn't have been proper. But I still felt bitterly disappointed and ashamed, not only for myself but for the Fanes, and perhaps most of all for The Comet, for the last event he would ever compete in, for a glorious career ended in dishonour, and all of it my fault. It was for The Comet that I could have wept.

'And now!' cried Felix Hissey, puffing out his chest grandly, 'I have the most *enormous* pleasure in being able to announce to you, the names of the successful candidates in the Hissey Training Scholarship for potential event riders!'

There was a flutter of anticipation amongst the crowd. Felix Hissey beamed. The chief appeared with a list of names which Felix Hissey took from him with a courtly little bow.

'Scholarships have been awarded to the following,' Felix Hissey announced. 'Selena Gibbons and Flame Thrower, Mary Ann Maddox and Edwin Drood, Phillip Hastings and

Master Facey Romford, Amanda Willis and Fox Me, Vivian Tintoft and Balthazar, and Alice Merryman and The Talisman.'

Roars of approval greeted this announcement. The Fanes and I turned to leave. None of us could take any more. But Felix Hissey was holding up his hands for silence and the cheering died away.

'There is one more successful candidate,' he informed us, 'and although the Hissey Training Scholarship provides for only six successful candidates and six have therefore been awarded; by a unanimous vote, and through some entirely exceptional circumstances, we have decided to award an extra scholarship this year.' Felix Hissey paused and drew a deep breath. 'That scholarship, for displaying outstanding potential and admirable determination in the face of difficult and quite extraordinary circumstances, goes to Elaine Elliot and Another Legend, owned by the Honorable Nigella and Henrietta Fane.'

The applause was simply deafening.

Sometime during the haze that followed, Lala Thornapple's nurse slipped an envelope into my anorak pocket.It contained a cheque for two and a half thousand pounds. With it was a short note.

> *Please don't refuse it* (it said).
> *Quentin Thornapple got a King's*
> *Ransome for Genesis when he sold*
> *him, and it's still only a fraction*
> *of his worth. Put it towards your*
> *training; finding Genesis again has*
> *made an old lady very happy.*

I handed the cheque to Henrietta. A year ago she had raised the money to buy Legend by selling the only valuable thing she possessed. Now I could repay her.

'Why are you giving it to me?' she wanted to know. 'I thought we had agreed that The Comet was your horse; it's your money, not mine.' She tried to give it back.

'No, no,' I said, 'it's for you. It's the money for Legend, repaid with interest.'

Henrietta stared down at the cheque in silence. She didn't look at all pleased.

'But we've enjoyed owning an eventer,' Nigella said. 'We don't want to be paid back. We would rather put the money into the Training Fund.'

'There's to be no more Training Fund,' I said, 'and no more fund raising. Now that I've paid you back for Legend and got a scholarship, I ought to be able to make it alone.' I was trying not to be emotional.

I knew there was no future in being sponsored by the Fanes any more, but it hurt, more than I would have believed possible, to have to say it.

There was a silence in the horse-box apart from The Comet, eating his hay.

'Are you leaving us, Elaine,' Nigella wondered, 'is that what you are trying to say?'

Now that she had asked, I couldn't deny it. 'I'd like to stay while Legend is recovering, and you will need help for the hunting season,' I said. 'The scholarship training doesn't begin until the spring. I would like to stay until then, if you'll have me.' It sounded awful, as if I was only staying because I hadn't anywhere better to go.

'Stay as long as you like,' Henrietta said, 'and leave when you like. I don't suppose we'll care, one way or another.' Despite the matter-of-fact tone of her voice, I knew she was hurt. She would have died though, rather than have shown it. She turned away and stuffed the cheque into her pocket. In the year and a half that I had known her she had been irritating and difficult, she had been suspicious of me and sometimes bad-tempered, but she had never blamed me for Legend's accident. Although he represented all of her wordly wealth, and she knew, as I knew, that it had been my fault, she had never said a word.

'Well, *I* rather think,' Nigella said sadly, 'that we'll all care very much indeed.'

Doreen came leaping into the horse-box, eating one of Felix Hissey's free currant buns. 'Nick Forster's waiting for you, Elaine,' she informed me. 'I told him I didn't know how long you'd be, but he said he'd wait all the same.'

I led The Comet down the ramp. He was to spend another night in the manor stables. It would have placed too much additional strain on his weary limbs to have expected him to travel home the same day.

Nick and I made our way slowly across the sheep-nibbled turf. The stiff, grey horse walked between us. From the ramp of the horse-box the Fanes watched his progress. None of us quite knew what was going to happen next.